SILENCE IN CENTER

JODY STUDDARD

Silence in Center

Cover Design: Jody Studdard

ISBN-13: 978-1496143679
ISBN-10: 1496143671

*For Derrick Coleman
and his awesome fans,
Erin and Riley*

The Tryout

Some days suck. May 15, 2013 was one of them. It started off okay but, as was sometimes the case, went downhill fast. I had a tryout with a fastpitch softball team called the Edmonds Express, which was a 14u select team from Edmonds, Washington, a small city about twenty minutes north of Seattle. I was really excited and a bit nervous because I had never played select softball before. I had played Little League for three years and I had made the Mill Creek All-Star team all three years I had played, but I had never tried to move up to the select level until then. The tryout was at a nice field in downtown Edmonds not too far from the city's high school. The team's coaches were friendly and outgoing, but it was still pretty intimidating, especially at first, because there were so many girls there. I'd guess around a hundred total, but there may have been more. The Express was usually a really good team, so a lot of girls from all around Seattle wanted to play for them and it was hard to win a spot unless you could really find a way to stand out and impress the coaches.

Which, at first, I thought I had done. There were six of them total, and they had us break into groups of ten girls each and go through various drills set up all over the field. My group was led by a man named James Harbaugh, who was a tall, lean man in his early forties with short, black hair, gray eyes, and a thick beard. I didn't know it at first, but later found out from some of the other girls he was the team's head coach. Originally, for some unknown reason, I thought he was one of the assistants. Anyway, he led us to the infield and had us form a single-file line at second base, then hit us a series of ground balls. Each girl got five, and I fielded them cleanly and whipped them over to first as fast as I could. An assistant was covering the base for us. When we were all done with our grounders, he had us jog out to the outfield and he hit fly balls to us. I was really excited because on my Little League team I was the center fielder so fly balls were my specialty. He hit me three in a row, which I caught easily. On one of them, I didn't even have to move. So then he decided to challenge me a little by hitting one to my left. I had to run about twenty feet to get to it, but I had always been pretty fast so I was able to catch it almost as easily as I caught the first three. Seeing I could catch balls on the run, he decided to really challenge me by hitting one deep into the outfield way over my head. I was forced to run all of the way to the outfield's warning track, and I ended up less than five feet away from the outfield fence itself, but I was able to make the catch anyway.

I was about as happy as I could be. Harbaugh smiled and nodded as I made the final catch, and I could tell he was impressed, at least a little. And he wasn't the only one. Sitting in the stands, watching everything intently, was my dad. He was a big sports fan and there was nothing he loved more than watching me play softball, so this was not only a big day for me but for him as well. He really wanted to see me win a spot and begin playing at the select level.

"Way to go, Melody," he called. "Well done."

From there, we moved to an adjacent field and did some hitting drills. Like always, we took turns, and Harbaugh pitched five balls to each of us. There were three girls who went before me, and they all did well. The first girl hit all five of her pitches sharply, including two that went all of the way to the warning track. The next girl fouled her first pitch away, but then made up for it by hitting the next four straight up the middle. The girl after her hit all five of her pitches into the outfield, and one of them hit and bounced off of the outfield fence. It was a great hit, and a great overall performance. But it wasn't as good as what I did. I hit my first three pitches straight up the middle, then finished by hitting the final two completely out of the park. The first cleared the fence by about five feet, and the second by about twenty. I was all smiles as I watched the second fly into the distance.

After hitting, Harbaugh got out a stopwatch and timed us running from home plate to first base. Each of us got two tries, which was good, since my first time was only so-so, but my second was really good, and I actually got the third best time of the day. After that, we called it good and wrapped things up, and I felt really confident. I felt like I had done everything possible to make the team, and I felt like I had a good chance of doing so. And I got even more excited when my dad and I were walking toward our car in the nearby parking lot and Harbaugh called out to us to wait up for a second. At the beginning of the tryout, he had told us he would not be making any roster decisions for a couple of days, since he liked to mull things over for a while, but I thought maybe he had changed his mind and had decided to offer me a spot immediately since I had done so well. My dad seemed equally excited and I could see a definite glint of hope in his eyes as Harbaugh jogged up to us. Unfortunately, however, our excitement, and our hopes for making the team, were short lived.

"Thanks for waiting," Harbaugh said. "I wanted to thank you for trying out, and Melody, you did a great job today. Unfortunately, however, I don't think I'm going to be able to offer you a spot on the team this year."

I was officially crushed. To be completely honest, I felt like my heart had been torn from my chest. I had really wanted to make the team, and since I had done so well, I thought I had.

And I wasn't the only one. My dad's eyes narrowed and his face got red. He couldn't believe what he had just heard.

"Really? Why? She did great in the field and she was one of the only girls who hit an out-of-the-parker. Actually, she hit two."

Harbaugh acknowledged the comment with a smile and a nod. "Those were some nice hits. No doubt about it. Especially the second one. I knew it was gone the minute it left her bat. But anyway, my real concern isn't her skills. She's clearly got plenty of them, especially for a girl who's never played select ball before. My concern is her disability."

The minute he said the word 'disability' my dad's eyes got big. "What do you mean?"

"We've never had a player with a disability on the team before and the assistant coaches and I aren't completely confident we know how to deal with it."

My dad, as had happened many times in the past when he had had to deal with similar situations, got defensive.

"She doesn't have a disability. She has a special need."

Harbaugh nodded. "Call it what you will, but I'm still not certain I'm comfortable dealing with it. I'm not certain I know how."

At this point, I should probably tell you what they were talking about. I have a severe hearing impairment, and as such I cannot hear much of anything without wearing a pair of specially designed hearing aids.

"Her Little League coaches never had any issues with it," my dad said.

"Good for them," Harbaugh said. "But Little League is a lot different than select ball. Things move quicker and are a lot more intense at the select level. I need to be able to shout commands and have my players respond to them immediately. I don't have time to do sign language."

My dad laughed. "She doesn't do sign language. With her hearing aids on, she can hear fine. Even from her spot in center field."

For a brief second, Harbaugh paused, as though he was contemplating things further and reevaluating his position, and I actually thought he might have a change of heart. But much to my chagrin, his opinion didn't waiver.

"It would probably be best if she tried another team. I hear the Broncos are looking for some players. They might be willing to give her a chance."

My dad, who never had much patience when dealing with people like Harbaugh, had heard enough.

"Fine. Thank you for your time today, Coach." He said the word 'coach' like it was venom in his mouth. "We'll contact the Broncos. But mark my words. You're going to regret this decision one day. It's just a matter of when and where."

He said it with such conviction it actually made Harbaugh's eyes get big for a second. Not knowing what else to do, Harbaugh turned and, without saying anything more, jogged back to the dugout where the other coaches were waiting for him.

My dad turned to me. "Come on, Melody. Let's go."

I had barely gotten into the car and was still struggling to get my seatbelt on, when I was flooded with emotion and started to cry. I just couldn't believe what had happened, nor how quickly things had changed. One minute, I thought I had made the team for sure, and the next minute I was sent packing.

My dad looked over and saw the tears running down my cheeks. He was irritated, but now his irritation had shifted from Harbaugh to me.

"What are you doing?"

"What do you mean?"

"Why are you crying?"

"Why wouldn't I? I just got rejected, for the third time in a week. And for the same reason each time."

It was true. The Express tryout was the third one I had had that week, and despite doing well at each, I had been rejected each time. The minute the coaches found out I had a hearing impairment, they got nervous and didn't know what to do about it. And then they reacted exactly like Harbaugh. They tried to be nice, and they tried to do their best to not hurt my feelings or offend me in any way, but they cut me anyway. And they did it because they made the same mistake so many people made when they were dealing with me. They assumed that since I needed hearing aids, I needed a lot of other things, too, and as such I was going to be a burden. But it wasn't like that at all. I didn't need anything special, other than a chance. And they didn't have anything to worry about when it came to me personally. I wouldn't let them down. I knew I wasn't the best softball player in the world, and I probably never would be, but I always tried hard, and I always gave one hundred percent. In three years of Little League play, I had never missed any games and I only missed one practice and that was because I caught the flu the week before, which was actually quite ironic since I had just gotten my yearly flu shot.

"We'll find you a team," my dad said. "You just have to be patient."

I had heard that before. After each tryout. "I've been patient. Three times now. Let's face it, dad, it's just not going to happen. Maybe I should just stick with Little League. My Little League coaches are used to dealing with me and they accept me for what I am. Maybe select ball is a bad idea."

My dad looked at me with a disappointed look on his face. "I thought you wanted to play select ball. Originally it was your idea."

I sighed. It was true, I did want to play select ball, badly, and it had indeed been my idea. "I guess some things just weren't meant to be."

As you can probably tell, I was so disappointed and so heartbroken I was contemplating giving up softball completely. Even Little League.

But my dad would hear none of it. "What are you doing?"

"What do you mean?"

"You're making excuses. What do I always tell you about making excuses?"

I sighed. Like most dads, my dad was extremely stubborn at times and when it came to my hearing impairment he was even more stubborn than normal. Over the years, he had refused to let me use it as an excuse and he had always insisted that despite needing hearing aids, I could do anything I wanted as long as I was willing to work hard, keep my chin up, and most importantly, never give up.

As such, I had no choice but to quote his motto, which I had heard seemingly a million times over the years.

"No excuses."

"Exactly. We'll find you a team. You just have to have some faith. Eventually, we'll find a coach who will be willing to give you a chance, and then you're going to become one of the best select players in the state. Just you wait and see."

I wanted to believe him, but I was still filled with uncertainty and doubt. As such, I didn't say anything more and instead just stared out the window at nothing in particular.

Without another word, my dad started the car, put it in gear, and we headed for home.

My Hitting Instructor

Some people probably think it would be terrible to be like me and have a hearing impairment, but to be honest it really wasn't that bad. Some days were frustrating, like the day of the Express tryout, but normally it didn't affect me too much and there was actually one thing about it that I really liked. Whenever I got frustrated, I could take my hearing aids off, plop down on my bed in the middle of my bedroom, and block everything out. Without my hearing aids on, I couldn't hear much of anything and the silence comforted me and helped me relax. And that's exactly what I was doing when my dad appeared unexpectedly and walked into my room. As soon as I realized he was there, I sat up, slipped my hearing aids back on, and asked what he wanted.

"Get your gear," he said. "Steve just called and he's got some time available."

He was referring to Steve Johns, my hitting instructor. Steve was a really nice guy, a former minor league baseball player who gave players from the area private lessons. At that point, I had been going to see him for about a year, usually once a week, but sometimes more depending on his availability.

So I climbed up, got my gear back on (which was kind of silly since I had just taken it off less than an hour before), grabbed my softball bag, and off we went. We met Steve at our normal place, a large industrial complex in south Seattle. It was quite a drive from our house in Mill Creek, but it was worth the hassle since Steve was such a great instructor. He was in his mid to late forties, and he had short, blonde hair, brown eyes, and a goatee, and like usual he was wearing gray sweatpants and a T-shirt. He was working with another girl when we arrived, so we had to wait about ten minutes before he finished, but as soon as he did he walked over and greeted us in his customary, jovial way.

"It's good to see you again, Miss Melody. How're you doing today?"

I was still a little bummed about the Express tryout, so my response wasn't nearly as enthusiastic as normal. "I'm okay."

He raised an eyebrow. He had been working with me for long enough to know when something wasn't quite right.

"What's wrong? Didn't your tryout go well? You had one today, didn't you?"

I was about to respond and tell him what had happened but my dad beat me to the punch.

"She did. And she did great. But she didn't get a spot anyway."

A puzzled look crossed Steve's face. "Why?"

"The coach wasn't comfortable working with a player with a hearing impairment."

"That's ridiculous. Her hearing impairment doesn't affect her ability to play. She's one of my best hitters."

"That's what I tried to tell him. But he wouldn't listen."

"Who was the coach?"

"James Harbaugh."

Steve's eyes got big the minute he heard the name. Clearly, he recognized it. "That explains a lot. To be honest, I've never liked Harbaugh. He's really tough on his players, especially his own daughter, and he gets out of control during games. I heard a story about a game last year, his team lost to the Eastside Angels, and he got so mad he yelled at his players and made them run wind sprints for an hour afterward. It's probably a good thing you didn't end up on that team, Miss Melody. Trust me, you wouldn't have liked it, not for long."

I was a little surprised because Harbaugh had actually seemed pretty nice to me during the tryout, until the end, of course, when he rejected me, and even then he had tried to be polite about it. At the same time, however, Steve would have known better. He was one of the most respected hitting instructors in the area and he knew just about everyone in the local softball scene.

He turned to me. "What are you going to do now?"

"I still want to play select ball but I'm not certain how. This was my third tryout and none of the teams have wanted me, so I'm not certain any will."

"Harbaugh mentioned a team called the Broncos," my dad said. "Do you know anything about them?"

Steve grimaced the minute he heard the name. "The Broncos aren't a good team. Their coaches are terrible. They're really just a dumping ground for the players Harbaugh doesn't want. Trust me, Miss Melody, you don't want to play for them."

"But I don't know who else to play for," I said. "And I can't really be choosy."

At that point, I could feel my frustration level rising again. The Broncos were pretty much my last hope, so if I couldn't play for them, I was pretty much out of luck. My career as a select player had ended even before it had begun.

Steve nodded, and it was clear he was contemplating something. "I've been thinking about this for a while now but I was a little hesitant to mention it since it's going to be a bit of a drive for you. I think you should try out for a team called Skyhawks Fastpitch. They're from Federal Way, so I know it's quite a way from your house in Mill Creek, but I know the coach and he's a really good guy. I guarantee he'll give you a fair shake. And if you do end up getting on the team you'll like it, I guarantee it. It's a good team with some really good girls."

My eyes got big, and I finally started to feel a little bit of hope again. It was true I wasn't looking forward to driving all of the way to Federal Way, since it was about an hour from our house in Mill Creek, but at the same time if it was my only option I was more than willing to give it a try.

Clearly, Steve saw the interest in my eyes, so he continued. "If you want I can give the coach a call right now and try to set up a tryout for you."

I really wanted him to do it, but I was hesitant since I didn't know how my dad would feel about driving all of the way to Federal Way, but clearly he didn't mind, either.

"Do it," he said. "Please."

As such, Steve pulled out his phone, dialed a number, then waited for an answer. It only took a few seconds for someone to respond, but to me it seemed like an eternity.

"Russell. It's me, Steve. How are you this fine day? Good. That's good. The kids? Sweet. Me? I'm fine. The wife is good and the kids are doing well. Except little Stevie, he got in another fight at school last week, so he got suspended for three days, but that's nothing new. The kid's a scrapper, I tell you. Anyway, I was calling because I wanted to know if you're still looking for some players for your roster this year."

My heart stopped. I couldn't wait for a response, and I desperately hoped it would be yes.

Luckily, and much to my relief, it was. "Good," Steve said. "I thought you'd say that." He turned to me. "He says he's always looking for good players."

He turned his attention back to the phone. "I've found one for you, Russell. I've been working with her for about a year now, and she's one of my best hitters. Up to this point, she's only played Little League but she's ready to move up. I'll vouch for her myself, she won't let you down." He paused briefly, clearly listening to what was being said on the other end. "Just a second, I'll ask." He turned to us. "He wants to know when you can do a tryout. He's free tomorrow afternoon if it works for you."

I nearly jumped for joy. And I wasn't the only one. My dad looked even more excited than I did. "It works," he said. "Just tell us when and where."

So that was that. Steve made the final arrangements, and before I knew it I had a new tryout set up for the very next day.

And unlike the first three, this one was awesome.

Another Try

The drive to Federal Way took even longer than I thought, since we hit some heavy traffic just south of Seattle, but I was excited anyway. I really wanted to play for a select team, so spending an hour in a car each way wasn't going to deter me in the least. My dad and I arrived at the tryout around 3:00 pm, and it was at a nice field not too far from the freeway. As soon as we got there, we were met by a tall, lean man who introduced himself as Russell Washington, and I liked him immediately. He was friendly and outgoing and his smile never left his face.

"Thank you for coming. I know it was a long drive for you."

"We don't mind," my dad said. "We're just grateful for the opportunity. We've been trying to hook up with a team for a while but things haven't gone too well."

"That surprises me. Steve told me Melody is quite a player. And Steve knows good players when he sees them. Teams should be fighting over her."

"I wish. Most coaches get skittish as soon as they find out she has a hearing impairment."

I held my breath. As far as I was concerned, that was the moment of truth. Russell's reaction would tell me everything I needed to know about how the tryout was going to go.

He raised an eyebrow. "Why is that an issue?"

"It shouldn't be," my dad said. "But to most, it is."

"Interesting. Well, just to be clear, it isn't with me. All I care about is whether you can play or not. If you can prove to me you can play, you're on the team. Understood?"

He turned and looked right at me.

At first, I was speechless. I didn't know what to think. Could it really be true? Had I finally found a coach who would give me a chance? My heart raced at the possibility.

"Understood?" he repeated. He clearly wanted me to answer.

"Understood," I said. "I can play, sir."

He laughed. "I prefer to be called Russell. Or coach, whatever you like. But not sir. It makes me feel old."

"Yes, sir. I mean, yes, Russell. Coach."

I was stumbling all over myself trying to say the right thing, and I clearly wasn't being very articulate, not in the least, but at the same time I just couldn't help myself. I was so overwhelmed with joy I could barely control myself.

Russell laughed. Clearly, he thought my enthusiasm was amusing. "Are you ready to get started? If so, grab your gear and join me on the field."

I looked all around, but much to my surprise I didn't see anyone else. My dad, Russell, and I were the only ones in the parking lot, and the nearby field was empty.

"Aren't there going to be other girls here? For the tryout?"

Up to that point, I had always thought tryouts were done in big groups, just like at the first three I had gone to.

Russell shook his head. "I like to do tryouts with each girl individually. That way I can see what I'm dealing with and I can give you a real chance to show what you're capable of. In big groups, it's too easy to miss things."

As far as I was concerned, it didn't get any better than that. I knew I could impress a coach if I could get a good opportunity. And one on one? It didn't get any better than that.

The next hour was one of the best experiences of my life. I grabbed my softball bag from the car and followed Russell onto the field, then ran through a series of drills with him. He worked me really hard, way harder than any of my Little League coaches ever had, and at one point I was completely covered in sweat, which was pretty gross, but I didn't care, not in the least. We did a bunch of grounders to start things off, and I fielded most of them cleanly, but I did miss two. One of them went straight through my legs – I hated when that happened. Regardless, Russell continued smiling the whole time and he complimented me whenever I made a nice play, and he said, "Good try" on the two I missed. As such, I felt really good about myself and my performance, and I started to feel even better once I moved to the outfield and started catching fly balls. Russell showed little mercy and hit every ball deeper and deeper into the outfield, but I hustled like never before and caught all but three of them. One of them hit the fence before I could get to it, but I was able to grab it on the rebound and throw it back to the infield quickly, which really seemed to impress Russell.

"Well done, Melody. That's exactly what I'm looking for. Even if you can't catch it on the fly, I want to see great effort anyway. Effort is what separates a good player from a great one. Understood?"

"Yes, sir. I mean, coach."

He smiled, then signaled for me to join him in the infield. "Now show me what you can do with that bat of yours."

I sprinted to the dugout, grabbed my bat and helmet, then ran back toward home plate. But before I got there, he stopped me in my tracks.

"Aren't you forgetting something, young lady?"

To be honest, I didn't know what he was talking about. As a result, I just stood there with a blank expression on my face.

"It's hot out here and you've been working really hard. You've got to be thirsty. Grab a drink before you pass out from dehydration."

It was true. I was really thirsty, but I wasn't going to do anything to jeopardize my chance of getting a spot on the team, so I hadn't planned to take a break until after we had finished. But now that he had said it was okay, I ran back to the dugout, grabbed my squirt bottle and took a long, much-needed drink, and man I was grateful. I was even thirstier than I had realized.

As soon as I finished, I started to put my batting helmet on, but Russell, who was standing at the edge of the dugout, stopped me and looked at me curiously.

"Do you mind if I ask? How do you have your hearing aids on? Do you have them taped to your head?"

I was kind of embarrassed since I didn't really like to talk about my hearing aids too much, especially with people I didn't know too well, but at the same time his question didn't seem offensive at all and really it just seemed like he was curious.

"Normally," I said, "they stay in place just fine, but sometimes I have issues with them when I'm running. So I tape them in place so they don't come off. And usually I wear a headband over them so no one can see the tape. But we were in a hurry today so I forgot my headband."

At that, my dad, who had been watching the tryout from the side, near the bleachers, walked up. Up to that point, he had been really happy with how things had been progressing, but his smile had been replaced with a concerned look.

"Is there an issue?"

Russell shook his head. "Not as far as I'm concerned. I was just curious, nothing more. Have you ever had one come off during a game?"

"Unfortunately," I said, "during my first year of Little League, I was running bases and my left one fell off. That was before I started taping them in place. I was running so hard I didn't even notice it at first. And then it was kind of embarrassing because the umpire had to stop the game and everyone, including the players on the other team, had to help me look for it."

"Why was that embarrassing?"

"You know. Everyone had to help me."

He shrugged. "That doesn't sound embarrassing to me. We all need help on occasion. Even us adults. Anyway, did you find it?"

I nodded. "It was near second base. It must have come out as I was rounding the base and heading for third. Luckily, it wasn't damaged and all I had to do was clean it off and everything was back to normal."

"Excellent. Excellent indeed."

The minute he said it, I felt like a ton of bricks had been lifted from my shoulders. When he had first brought up the subject and asked me about my hearing aids, I was worried he was asking about them so he could determine if it really was a good idea to have a girl like me on the team. But he wasn't. Like I had originally thought, and like he had told my dad, he was curious and nothing more.

A few seconds later, we headed back onto the field and resumed the tryout. I took my place at home plate, and he went to the pitching circle with a bucket of balls in one hand, and he pitched about twenty of them to me. To be honest, I didn't do quite as well as I would have liked, and I definitely didn't do as well as I had done at the Express tryout, but even so I still think he was pleased with my performance. Of the twenty pitches, I hit twelve into the outfield, including four that went straight up the middle and three that bounced off of the outfield fence.

Once we finished hitting, Russell rounded up his stuff and took it back to his car, which was parked just a couple of stalls away from ours. At first, I was a little nervous since he hadn't said much as he had walked away from me, so I really didn't know what was going to happen next. After placing his equipment in his car, he returned with something in his hand, but I couldn't tell what it was until he reached out and handed it to me. Much to my delight, it was a pair of pants and a light blue jersey. The jersey had silver lettering on the front and the number forty on the back.

"Welcome to the Skyhawks."

Skyhawks Fastpitch

I was pretty much on top of the world the entire drive home. I had finally found myself a team, and I was so excited I couldn't wait to text my friends and tell them all about it. My dad was equally excited, and he called Steve to tell him what had happened, and he thanked him repeatedly for setting the whole thing up for us. As soon as I got home, I couldn't help but go into the bathroom and try on my new uniform and it looked awesome. I stood in front of the mirror for at least an hour admiring it and I loved everything about it. The pants were dark blue and they went perfectly with the jersey, especially since they had light blue stripes that went down their sides. My mom thought I was silly when she called me to dinner and I came down still wearing my uniform, and I even ate dinner in it, but at the same time she agreed it looked good and it fit perfectly.

"I can't wait to see you wearing it during a game," my dad said. "That will be awesome."

"Totally," I said.

My first practice was three days later, at the same park in Federal Way where I had done my tryout with Russell, and once again the drive was long and tiring, but it didn't dampen my enthusiasm at all. I couldn't wait to meet my new teammates and get my career as a big shot select softball player underway. Unfortunately for me, however, the practice didn't start as well as I had hoped. Select ball was much faster and much more competitive than Little League, and at first I couldn't believe how hard the other girls could throw the ball, nor how far they could hit it. In addition, the Skyhawks were a 16u team, so their players were fifteen and sixteen, and since I was only fourteen I was the youngest girl on the entire team. I felt like a midget among giants. Russell was as friendly as ever and he introduced me to everyone and tried his best to help me fit in, but I was pretty intimidated. Things got even worse when we lined up to do some grounders in the infield and I tripped over my own feet and face-planted right in front of everyone (I was usually a pretty coordinated person, but every once in a while, especially when I got nervous, I had issues). I jumped up as fast as I could and tried to save some face, but the first thing I saw was the Skyhawks' main pitcher, who was a tall, thin girl named Riley Westmore, looking straight at me, and she did not look impressed, not in the least. She shook her head, then turned to a girl next to her, who I later learned was the team's shortstop, and said, "This is our new center fielder? Wonderful."

I tried my best to ignore what she had said and block it from my mind, and luckily for me I did pretty well for the rest of the drill. When it was my turn, Russell hit me four grounders in a row and I fielded each of them cleanly and tossed them to the girl who was covering first base.

After grounders, we did some base running and I learned another valuable lesson. Select players were fast. In Little League, I was easily the fastest girl on my team, and only one girl, our shortstop, ever came close to beating me. But on the Skyhawks, I finished each sprint in fourth to last place, and the only players I beat were the two catchers and one outfielder. So I was a little disheartened, to say the least, and batting drills didn't help me any, either. We did a few exercises with plastic balls to warm up, then took turns as Riley pitched to us. Her first pitch blew by me so fast I didn't even have time to swing at it. I had never seen a pitch like that before. Her second pitch looked like nothing but a bright, yellow blur. Her third was the first one I actually managed to swing at, but even so I missed it by a mile. I managed to hit her fourth pitch, a little, but I only got the bottom half of it and it went straight back and bounced off of the backstop with a loud clang.

She yelled at me from her spot in the pitching circle.

"Keep your chin down, Melody. And your hands up. Don't drop them or I'll strike you out all day. Got it?"

I was pretty intimidated, since she was an absolute fireball of a girl, but I was grateful for the advice, so I called back and tried to thank her. "Got it. Thanks, Riley."

She smiled, then repeated what I had said.

"Got it. Thanks, Riley."

I grimaced the minute she said it, since she had said it exactly the way I had -- in other words, she had imitated me. Some of the girls who were nearby started to chuckle, but Russell brought the whole thing to a quick and thankful end with one brisk remark.

"I'll have none of that. Understood?"

At first, there was no response, so he turned directly to Riley.

"Understood?"

"Whatever." She rolled her eyes but didn't say anything more.

At this point, I should probably explain to you what had happened. Since I couldn't hear perfectly, even with my hearing aids on, I couldn't speak like everyone else. To me I sounded just fine, and once people got used to hearing me they had no problem understanding me at all, but some people, especially young children, thought I sounded funny. Despite seeing countless speech therapists over the years, I still had a really hard time controlling my voice's volume and pitch, and as such some people said it sounded like I was speaking inside of a concrete tunnel. One time, when I was five, a little boy who lived down the street said I sounded like a cartoon character, and I got so mad at him for saying it I actually beat him up, which led to me getting grounded for a week for doing it. Regardless, I had been teased and picked on countless times over the years, and at first it really hurt my feelings, but not so much as the years passed by. I guess I just got numb to it after a while. I would just do my best to shrug it off and move along, and that's what I did with Riley. I completely blocked out the fact she had made fun of me, and instead I focused on the advice she had given me. I kept my hands up, and my chin down, and the results were exactly what I wanted. I hit her next pitch into center field, then hit the one after that sharply up the middle.

"Very nice, Melody," Russell said. "Way to finish strong. Now head out and do some work with the outfielders."

From that point forward I had nothing but fun. Since I'm a center fielder, outfield is where I belong and it's where I feel the most comfortable. I met the team's other outfielders, including a stocky blonde with freckles named Sophia Davidson and a tall, lean girl named Kaitlin Jones (Kaitlin had the prettiest red hair I had ever seen). Sophia was the right fielder, and Kaitlin was the left fielder, and both of them were fifteen. They were all smiles the minute I joined them.

"It's nice to meet you," Sophia said. "We've been wondering for a while when Russell was going to find us a new center fielder. The last one moved to California with her family."

"It's nice to be here," I said. "I'm trying my best to fit in but I'll be honest I'm a little nervous today so I'm sorry if I'm acting a little weird."

"Who wouldn't be nervous?" Kaitlin asked. "Everyone's nervous on their first day with a new team. You should have seen me last year during my first practice. I was a wreck. I didn't hit a single one of Riley's pitches. You hit two, so you did a lot better than me."

"I wasn't much better on my first day," Sophia said. "I made back-to-back errors during infield drills. Then I dropped a fly ball in the outfield. It was a total disaster. So don't worry about it. No matter how you do today, it's no big deal and in no time you'll feel like you've been part of the team forever."

"I'm not certain Riley likes me."

"Don't worry about her," Kaitlin said. "She's always tough on the new girls. But she means no harm and if you give her a chance you'll see she's one of the best teammates you could ever have."

"Really?" I found that pretty hard to believe since she had actually gone to the extent of picking on me. "She seems pretty intimidating to me."

"Only at first," Sophia said. "But you'll see. Once you win her over, and trust me you will, you'll have a friend for life."

I didn't really know what Sophia meant by 'win her over' but at the same time I didn't really care. To be honest, I was just happy to have found some girls who were open and friendly toward me. Unfortunately, however, we didn't get much more time to speak since Russell walked over and started hitting fly balls to us. We took turns and I caught all five that were hit my way. Sophia and Kaitlin cheered as I caught the final one, since I had to run all of the way across the warning track and reach over the outfield fence in order to get it.

"You've never played select ball before?" Kaitlin asked.

I shook my head. "No. Just Little League."

"You could have fooled me. You look like a select player to me. And a darn good one at that."

Thanks to her comment, I was the happiest girl on the planet.

Summer League

My second practice with the Skyhawks was even better than the first. The pitcher, Riley, was still a little standoffish and not too friendly, but everyone else was great. I spent most of my time working with the other outfielders, Sophia and Kaitlin, but also spent some time working with the shortstop, who was a small, thin girl named Erin Williams. Erin was sixteen so she was one of the oldest girls on the team, and she was also the team's captain, so she gave me a lot of tips, advice, and general guidance. At one point during our batting drills, she saw I was struggling with my bunts, so she walked over and helped me out.

"You've got to keep the end of your bat up at all times. No matter how far the ball drops, no matter how low it goes, you can never let the end of the bat fall below it."

"But how do I get to the low ones?"

Low pitches were the ones I had been struggling with. Every time I tried to get one, I would just hit it straight up into the air where the catcher would snag it easily.

"You've got to bend your knees. Lower the bat by lowering yourself."

I gave it a try. Erin tossed me a ball, really low, and I tried to bunt it like she had said. It felt really awkward at first, and I missed the first one miserably, but the second one I hit just fine, and it went right down the first base foul line, right where I wanted. The third one was even better, and it went down the third base foul line.

"Good," Erin said. "That's exactly how you do it. You'll be terrorizing pitchers in no time."

From there, we worked on different drills, but the real highlight of practice didn't occur until Russell called for a break, gathered us up, and made a big announcement.

"It's still a few weeks away but I wanted to let you all know I registered us for Seattle's Summer League again this year."

As soon as he made the announcement, everyone except me cheered. I would have cheered, too, but to be honest I didn't know what he was talking about. I had never heard of Seattle Summer League before.

Russell was about to explain it to me but Kaitlin cut him off.

"It's the funnest tournament of the year. We did it last year and we made it all of the way to the semifinals. This year I think we can win it all."

Her eyes were filled with excitement and anticipation as she said it.

"Okay," I said. "But what is it?"

At that, Russell took over and his description was a little more thorough than Kaitlin's. "It's a tournament played for four consecutive weeks starting June 15. There are sixteen teams total, and each team plays four games per week, two on Tuesday and two on Thursday, for the first three weeks. During the fourth week, the playoffs begin, and from there you keep playing until you lose a game. Once you lose a game, you're eliminated and your tournament is over."

Kaitlin couldn't contain her excitement any longer.

"Tell her the good part. Tell her where the championship is."

Russell laughed. Clearly, he knew Kaitlin well and he knew she had a hard time controlling herself, especially when she really liked something. "The championship is in Husky Stadium."

The minute he said it, my heart stopped. I couldn't believe what I had just heard. Husky Stadium was the home field of the University of Washington's softball team. I had been there before, a couple of times, to see the Huskies play Stanford and UCLA (the Huskies won both games). It was the nicest softball field I had ever seen, with grandstands for the fans, concession stands with food and drinks, lights so you could play at night, and grass that was so lush it looked like a putting green at a fancy golf course.

"Really? We get to play in Husky Stadium?" I couldn't believe it. I had never pictured myself playing on a field as nice as that before.

"We do," Russell said, "but only if we can make it to the championship game. Last year we got close, like Kaitlin said all of the way to the semifinals, but this year I think we can make it, but only if you ladies are willing to buckle down and work hard."

He didn't have anything to worry about, at least not with me. I would have practiced non-stop from then until the championship game if that was what it took to get to play in Husky Stadium. To me, playing in Husky Stadium was like a dream come true.

"But it's not going to be easy," Russell said. "There are a lot of good teams in the tournament this year, including the Devils."

The minute he said the word 'Devils' the girls got quiet.

"I hate them," Riley said.

Once again, I was completely in the dark. I guess that was the bad thing about being the new girl. Luckily, however, Erin saw the look on my face and offered an explanation.

"The Devils are a team from Tacoma. Usually, they're really good, and they're the team that eliminated us from the tournament last year. But that's not the reason we dislike them so much."

I raised an eyebrow as I waited for her to continue. But much to my surprise, she wasn't the one to do so. Riley was.

"I tried out for them three years ago. And I made the team. The coach told me I was going to be one of their 'star' pitchers and of course I was really excited. But then a week later, a new girl came along, another pitcher, and apparently they liked her better than me so they cut me and kept her. I never got to play a single game with them."

I didn't know what to say. That sounded so unfair to me.

"Once a team picked a girl and told her she was on the team, I thought they were supposed to keep her for the whole season."

"They're supposed to," Russell said, "but the Devils' coach is a man named Scott Franklin and he pretty much does whatever he wants, whether it's fair to his players or not. His main concern is winning, not fairness."

I was in shock. I couldn't imagine how horrible that must have been for Riley. It would have been like if Russell came up to me after practice and told me he didn't want me on the Skyhawks anymore. I would have been crushed. I would have jumped off of the nearest bridge.

"So we really want to beat them this year," Erin said, "so we can get some payback for Riley. We almost did it last year but they came back and won in the final inning. I still haven't gotten over it. We were so close."

"We can beat them this year," Riley said. "I know we can. We're better than ever."

Being a good coach, Russell never missed a chance to fire us up and get us motivated.

"You bet we are. Let me hear it, ladies. Can we do it? Can we beat the Devils?"

"We can," we yelled.

A disgusted look appeared on his face.

"Is that the best you can do? I can't hear you."

"We can."

That time, we were twice as loud as before. Maybe louder. I almost had to turn down my hearing aids it was so loud.

We officially had a mission. We were going to beat the Devils. We were going to do it for Riley.

The Season Begins

The next two weeks were two of the funnest, but toughest, weeks I had ever had. Russell was a great coach, but he worked us hard. Every practice started with a twenty-minute jog and ended with thirty minutes of wind sprints. And if that wasn't enough, at the midpoint we had to do numerous sets of pushups, crunches, and other strength building exercises. On one day, we did so many squats I didn't think my thighs would ever recover, and the next day I was so sore I could barely get out of bed. Even so, I loved every minute of it, and in a two-week period I improved more than I ever thought possible. Even more importantly, however, I got comfortable. Within no time, I had been fully integrated into the team and, much to my delight, nobody thought of me as the new girl anymore. Well, nobody but Riley. She still seemed a little standoffish, but not overly so, so I wasn't too worried about her. After all, some people just took a little longer to accept new teammates than others.

Anyway, before I could blink an eye the big day had finally arrived. The first day of Seattle's Summer League. We had two games, back-to-back, and they were both at Lower Woodland Park in north Seattle, just to the south of Green

Lake. It was a nice, summer day, with just a little cloud cover. We were all really excited, and a little nervous, especially me since it was my first game as a select player. For the first time, I got to wear my uniform (like most teams, we didn't wear our uniforms at practice), and I went all out and even got some blue and silver sparkles to put on my face so I'd look really festive. We arrived at the game about an hour early, did warm-ups with Russell, then took to the field like a bunch of Roman gladiators heading for the Colosseum. Our first game was against a team from Redmond called the Mustangs, and they wore bright red uniforms with yellow stripes. I'll give them credit; they looked sharp, but they didn't look nearly as good as us. Everyone knows blue uniforms are better than red ones. I took my place in center field, with Kaitlin and Sophia to my sides, and basically just watched for the first couple of innings. As I had learned during the previous two weeks, Riley was a great pitcher, and she basically just mowed down the first two Mustang batters. They looked completely overwhelmed. Riley threw a bunch of different pitches, and she threw them all well, but her best by far was a nasty changeup that fooled batters ninety percent of the time. It was almost twenty miles per hour slower than her other pitches, and as such most batters ended up swinging way too soon. Unlike the Mustang's first two hitters, however, who both struck out, the Mustang's third batter, who was a large, power hitting lefty named Julia Richardson, actually managed to hit one of Riley's pitches, but the ball went straight to Erin at short. Erin scooped it up and threw it to first for a nice, easy out.

The second inning was more of the same. Riley struck out the first batter, this time with a nasty riseball, then got the next two batters to pop up to our first baseman, Kaylee Smith, and our third baseman, Olivia Jennings. Things didn't get really interesting, at least as far as I was concerned, until the third inning. That was when I got to make my first play. The leadoff batter hit Riley's first pitch, and she hit it hard, but straight to me in center so all I had to do was put my mitt up and grab it.

It was an easy play and anyone could have done it, but to me it was huge. It was the first time I had made a contribution during a game, and as such I felt like a million dollars. Kaitlin shouted, "Nice catch," Kaylee yelled, "Way to be," and Russell (from the dugout) cheered loudly.

If that wasn't good enough, my contributions didn't end there. My first chance to bat happened the next inning, and when I stepped up to the plate we had no outs and Kaitlin on first (she hit a sweet single right past the Mustang's second baseman). Russell gave me the signal to lay down a sacrifice bunt, and I did exactly what Erin had taught me in practice. I kept the end of my bat up, dropped down using my knees, and bunted the ball right down the third base foul line. The third baseman rushed in, grabbed the ball, and threw it to first in time to get me, but everyone cheered anyway because I had done exactly what Russell had wanted me to do – I had sacrificed myself to move Kaitlin to second. As I returned to the dugout, everyone patted me on the back and Erin said, "Nicely done, Melody." Two batters later, Kaitlin scored when Riley lined a shot into left center, and just like that we were ahead 1-0.

The score remained the same until the fifth inning, when Erin led things off with a double, then Kaylee followed with a massive blast to left. For a second, I thought it was going to be a home run, but instead it hit the wall and bounced to one side. Erin scored easily, and Kaylee ended up on third with a standup triple. She scored shortly thereafter when Olivia hit a single straight up the middle. As such, we were leading 3-0 when I got my next chance to bat. The Mustang's pitcher, who was a lanky girl with long, blonde bangs, got two quick strikes on me, then tried to finish me off with a curveball over the outside edge of the plate. My hitting instructor, Steve, would have been so proud of me since I did exactly what he had always instructed me to do when facing a nasty pitch like that. I waited as long as possible, then reached out and lined it down the first base foul line. The first baseman lunged at it, but she wasn't able to get to it in time, so it raced past her into right field. I ran as quickly as I could, and before I knew it I was standing on first base, and all of my teammates were cheering and chanting my name.

And they weren't the only ones. My parents were in the stands, watching attentively, and they were pretty happy, too. My dad was nothing but smiles.

"Way to go, Melody," he called.

What a rush. As far as I was concerned, there was nothing better than getting a hit during a softball game. It wasn't easy to do, and it took a lot of hard work beforehand, but when you did it, it made you feel like the champion of the world.

Unfortunately, however, I didn't get to enjoy being the champion of the world for long. The next batter, Sophia, hit a shot to the gap in left center, and as such I was off to the races. I was going to call it good and stop at third but then I saw Russell waving for me to head home so I ran for all I was worth. The Mustang's center fielder grabbed the ball and tried to throw me out at the plate, but the ball got there a second too late and I slid under the tag.

As such, the rout was on. It was 5-0, and everyone cheered and patted me on the back as I made my way into the dugout. Even Riley, who was the least friendly person on the team, gave me a compliment.

"Nice hustle, kid."

The final score was 7-0 and we were ecstatic. Our first game of the season had come and gone, and we had prevailed easily. Unfortunately, however, our victory celebration was short-lived because we weren't done for the day. We still had a second game and it was against a team called Seattle Fastpitch. Our backup pitcher, Megan Morgan, started the game for us, and Riley took over at second. Despite being Riley's backup, Megan was a good pitcher, too, and she did a great job. She only gave up three hits the entire game, and we cruised to another victory, this time 5-1. Erin got two doubles, Riley hit a massive triple into left center, and Kaitlin added a solo homer. I went one for three with a single up the middle, and I would have had another but I got robbed when Seattle Fastpitch's shortstop made a great diving catch. In the field, I made three good plays, including one catch on the run in deep center.

As such, I was all smiles as my parents and I loaded my stuff into the car and headed for home. My long-awaited debut as a select softball player had finally arrived and as far as I was concerned it had been a smashing success.

Nightmares

That night, my fun ended, at least temporarily, because I had a nightmare. To you, a nightmare might not seem like that big of a deal since everyone has them on occasion, but to me it was. My nightmare was the same one I had had countless times over the years, and it was absolutely terrifying because it was a nightmare in which I relived the worst day of my life.

The day I lost my hearing.

I haven't told you yet, but I didn't always have a hearing impairment. When I was young, I had normal hearing, just like most people do, and I could hear things as cleanly and as clearly as anyone. But all of that changed on one fateful day when I was four. I hadn't been feeling well for a couple of days beforehand, but everyone, including my mom and dad, thought it was nothing more than a cold or maybe even a mild case of the flu. But I awoke that morning feeling worse than ever and within an hour, things had gone from bad to horrible. My temperature skyrocketed and at one point I tried to walk across the room but I got so dizzy I stumbled to the left and fell. I was sweating so badly my shirt was completely soaked. My mom found me lying on the floor and screamed for my dad, who ran into the room, scooped me up, and carried me to his car in the garage. He put me in the backseat, and my mom jumped in with me and held me tightly as he drove like a madman to the hospital. I had never seen him drive like that before. He was going at least fifty miles per hour in a thirty-five mile per hour zone and he was weaving in and out of traffic like he was crazy. In the meantime, my mom was crying like a baby and I was pretty much delirious (for a while, it seemed like the entire world was spinning around me, then everything started moving in slow motion, then everything started to turn dark and hazy). At one point we got pulled over by a police car but as soon as the officer saw me in the backseat he knew there was something wrong and he said, "Follow me" and led us straight to the hospital. With him in front of us, and with his lights flashing and his sirens blaring, we made it there quickly. A team of doctors, paramedics, and nurses were waiting for us upon arrival and they put me on a stretcher and wheeled me into a treatment room as fast as they could. They started injecting me with a bunch of needles and they hooked me to several machines including one that had a million tubes coming out of it. There were people everywhere and they were rushing around and shouting things to one another and normally it would have been pretty scary, but I was pretty much history at that point. The last thing I heard before I blacked out was a doctor shouting, "We're losing her."

Luckily for me, I lived, but I was in the hospital for over a month afterward. My fever had caused my brain to swell temporarily and that swelling had led to permanent brain damage that somehow affected my hearing. I never really understood what had happened and to be honest I'm not certain the doctors understood, either. They gave me numerous explanations, but the explanations varied, and some of them involved big words I didn't understand. Ultimately, however, I guess it didn't matter. What had happened had happened. I've always been grateful, however, since I lived, and if all I had to do was sacrifice some of my hearing to do so, well that was a trade I would make any day. Granted, it wasn't easy, especially the first year or so, and I'll admit there were some days where I struggled and felt sorry for myself and a few days where I cried my eyes out. Luckily, however, those days slowly faded away and I found a way to adapt and move on. I had to learn how to live with only about five percent of my hearing, but thanks to my doctors, audiologists, otolaryngologists, and other hearing specialists, I was able to do so.

It should also be noted I got some help from a therapist, to help me deal with the psychological and emotional aspects of losing my hearing, and like everyone she was very knowledgeable and nice, but there was one thing she could never help me conquer: the nightmares. They happened on occasion, with no warning whatsoever, and when they did they were so vivid and so scary they terrified me and I could never get back to sleep afterward. As such, on that particular night I had no choice but to do what I had always done when they happened. I turned on the lamp next to my bed, grabbed the first book I could find (*Escape from Dinosaur Planet*), and spent the rest of the night reading it.

Summer League Continues

Two days later, we had our next pair of Summer League games. The first game was against a team from Tacoma called the Tide, and it turned out to be much more challenging than our first two games had been. The Tide was a good team, and their girls were huge. They made us look tiny by comparison. Even so, we weren't intimidated, especially our older girls like Riley and Erin. Riley pitched and did a great job. The Tide managed to get a few hits off of her, here and there, and they scored a run in the bottom of the third, but other than that she held them in check. In the meantime, we scored a run of our own in the second inning when Kaitlin hit a solo home run, then we added three more in the fifth when Erin and Olivia hit back-to-back doubles. The final score was 4-1, and I went two for four with two singles. In the field, I made a pair of catches.

The next game, however, was a different story. It was against a team from Woodinville called the Wolves, and they were really good. Megan pitched for us and she gave up two runs in the first, then two more in the third, and before we knew it we were losing 4-0. We got two of the runs back in the bottom of the fifth when Erin hit a massive home run to center, but that was the best we could do. We ended up losing 5-2 and I didn't get any hits at all. I ended up zero for four, with two weak flies to center, a groundout to second, and a strikeout.

We were all pretty disappointed, since it was our first loss of the season and nobody liked losing, but at the same time nobody got too upset. The first three weeks of Summer League were "pool play" and were pretty much just for fun. Things didn't get really serious until the fourth week when the playoffs began. At that point, if we lost a game, our dreams of reaching the championship game and playing in Husky Stadium would be dashed.

I didn't like the thought of that at all.

The Leavenworth Invite

The following weekend was an exciting and unforgettable one for me. My team, the Skyhawks, played most of its games as part of Seattle's Summer League and winning the Summer League championship was our primary goal for the year, but every once in a while Russell mixed things up and we played in other tournaments as well. That particular weekend, we were playing in a tournament called the Leavenworth Invite and I was really excited because it was the first time I had ever been on a softball road trip. Leavenworth was a small city in eastern Washington about two hours from Seattle, just over the mountains, and the tournament lasted all weekend so there was no way to drive back and forth between games. As such, our team's manager, who is actually Russell's sister, Rochelle, made arrangements and rented a bunch of rooms for us in a hotel in downtown Leavenworth. My dad and I drove over on Friday night, after he got home from work, and most of the team was already there by the time we arrived (some of them, including Russell, greeted us in the hotel's parking lot as we pulled up). Leavenworth was a gorgeous city, just off of Interstate 2, and its buildings had facades that made the entire place look like a traditional Bavarian village. It reminded me of something out of a Brothers Grimm fairy tale. Our hotel was named the Obertal and was on the main street that ran through town, and there were restaurants, shops, and stores of all types within walking distance, which was nice for us girls since few of us were old enough to drive. We checked in, took our stuff up to our rooms, then headed to a restaurant called Gustav's for dinner. As far as I was concerned, it was a great place, since it was lively and bustling with activity and it served German food, which I really liked. I ordered my favorite, bratwurst with extra sauerkraut. We girls sat at one table, and Russell, the assistant coaches, and the dads sat at another, and it was a fun time. Our table really wasn't big enough for all of us but we were resourceful and made it work anyway, which really just meant we pushed our chairs together as tightly as possible. Everyone talked and joked as we ate and since I was new to the team it was a great opportunity for me to learn a little more about everyone, including what they liked and where they went to school. I also found out that several of them, especially the older girls like Erin and Olivia, had boyfriends, and everyone got really animated when Riley announced she had finally gone out with a boy named Jason Jones. Apparently, she had had the hots for him for quite a while and he had finally asked her out just the night before.

They had gone to a movie and had had a good time.

Unfortunately, however, things soured a little, at least as far as I was concerned, just after the waitress cleared our dinner plates and brought us dessert (I got chocolate covered strawberries, with white chocolate, and they were to die for). Erin, who was seated directly across from me, looked over and said, "Tell us a little about you, Melody. We haven't known you for long so we don't know much about you."

I was instantly uncomfortable since I normally didn't like to have the focus on me, especially in an environment like that when I was still getting to know everyone, but I did my best anyway since I really liked the team and wanted to fit in as well as possible.

"What do you want to know?"

"Anything. Where do you go to school?"

"Jackson."

Most of the girls had puzzled expressions on their faces. Since most of them were from south of Seattle, they hadn't heard of Jackson before.

"It's in Mill Creek. Just north of Seattle. Near Everett."

They nodded but I could still tell they had no idea where Jackson was.

"What grade are you in?" Kaylee asked.

"I'm a freshman."

"Have you started driving yet?" Erin asked.

"Not yet." I shot a glance across the room, at the table where Russell and the dads sat. Like always, they were talking about sports, cars, and other guy stuff. "I'm hoping to start soon. As soon as I can talk my dad into it."

"That's the hard part. Dads can be so difficult at times."

Every girl at the table nodded. But then Riley looked at Erin and said, "What are you talking about? Your dad is the greatest. He spoils you rotten."

Erin's eyes got big. "No way. He's a beast. You're the one who's spoiled."

"No way."

"Yes way. Who got a car for her Sweet Sixteen?"

Riley's eyes got big and apparently she decided to concede the point once Erin mentioned her car. "I may be spoiled a little. But just a little."

Everyone laughed. Things were quiet for a few seconds as everyone returned to their desserts, but then the focus came back to me. Our catcher, Danielle Watson, who was a tall, pretty girl with the nicest eyes I had ever seen, turned to me and said, "Melody, there's something I've wanted to ask you, and I know some of the other girls have been curious about it, too, but I'm not really certain how to ask. None of us have ever had a deaf teammate before, or even known anyone who was deaf, so we were wondering what it's like."

My entire body got rigid as she asked the question. This was one thing I had always hated.

I had always hated being singled out because I was the 'deaf girl.' And I had always hated how people had to be so curious and they had to know so much about it. Couldn't they see I would rather not discuss it?

Apparently, however, they couldn't, because the whole table had gone completely silent and they were all looking right at me. Clearly, they all wanted to know the answer to Danielle's question and it made me wonder if it had been something they had been discussing amongst themselves.

Like always, I didn't want to talk about it, but I decided to humor them since I really wanted to win them over and fit in as well as I could.

"It's not too bad. As you can see, I can do pretty much the same things as you."

"How is it you can hear if you're deaf?"

"I'm not fully deaf. I can still hear a little. Really, I'm just hearing impaired."

"Is that the term we're supposed to use?" Erin asked. "Hearing impaired? I never know nowadays since it seems like they change the terms all of the time to make them politically correct and not offend anyone. Like handicapped. We're not supposed to use that term any more either, right? Or are we?"

Everyone laughed. No one knew if we were supposed to use the term or not.

I smiled. "To be honest, I don't really care what you call me. Deaf, hearing impaired, handicapped, special needs, I've heard them all over the years. To me, the term is irrelevant. But what matters is how you treat me. I don't want you to feel sorry for me, since there is nothing to feel sorry about, and I want you to treat me just like the rest of you."

"Do people treat you differently?" Danielle asked.

I nodded. "Most people do. The funniest ones are the ones who are too nice. Some people, once they learn I have a hearing impairment, they go out of their way to make special accommodations for me and trust me it gets old fast. One year, on the first day of class, a teacher tried to communicate with me using sign language. It was really funny since I don't know sign language."

"Really?" Sophia asked. "Why is that? Why don't you know sign language?"

I shrugged. "Talking is easier."

"I thought all people who had hearing impairments were taught sign language," Erin said.

"Most are. And I was taught it, too, when I was young and I went to a school for kids who are deaf. But I forgot it all years ago."

"You went to a school for deaf kids?" Sophia asked.

I nodded. "When I was five. But only for a year. Then my dad decided I didn't need it so he mainstreamed me."

"Mainstreamed?" Riley asked. Clearly, she had never heard the term before. And from the looks on the other girls' faces I could tell they hadn't heard it, either.

"He sent me to a normal school. A public school. Like the ones you go to."

"Has that been tough?" Danielle asked. "Going to a public school with a hearing impairment?"

"Sometimes. I've had good days and bad days. But don't we all?"

They all nodded. Several of them even snickered as soon as I made the comment.

"Some weeks," Riley said, "I have more bad days than good."

Everyone laughed.

"Can I see one of your hearing aids?" Danielle asked. "I've never seen one before. Is it like a pair of headphones?"

I had actually calmed down quite a bit, since it was clear to me the girls meant no harm by their questions. They weren't teasing me at all and they weren't being mean in any way. Quite to the contrary, they were curious and nothing more (just like Russell had been on the day of my tryout). As such, I decided it was probably the best chance I would ever get to bond with them and teach them more about me. I reached up and removed my left hearing aid, then handed it to Danielle so she could see it. Like most behind-the-ear hearing aids, it was small and curved, with one piece that went into my ear (into the canal itself), and another piece that wrapped around the back of my earlobe. The piece that wrapped around my earlobe was the part that contained the hearing aid's amplifier, speaker, microphone, and battery. It was also the part I had to tape to the side of my head when I did anything athletic. Danielle looked at it curiously for a few seconds, then handed it to Erin so she could look at it, then she passed it to Riley, then she passed it to the next girl, and so on and so forth. It kind of reminded me of show and tell day back in first grade. My hearing aid went from girl to girl, and before it finally got back to me, everyone had gotten a chance to look at it and examine it carefully.

"It seems pretty neat to me," Erin said. "Is it form fitted?"

"It is. My hearing specialist used a mold of my ear to get it just right. Even so, I have to be careful since it still falls off on occasion."

"Can you adjust its volume?" Sophia asked. "And turn it up and down like a set of headphones?"

"I can. And sometimes I do. Some days, when I'm in class, if too many people start talking all at once, my hearing aids have a hard time discerning the voices and they all blend together. Everything seems like a garbled, incomprehensible mess, so it doesn't do me any good to listen to it."

My hearing aid had finally made its way back to me and I was thankful it had. When I wore only one, it irritated me and made me uncomfortable. I'm not exactly certain why and the only explanation my hearing specialist had for it was it had something to do with the fact I could only hear things from one direction, which I wasn't used to, and as such it disoriented and confused me. Sometimes, it even made me dizzy.

For a brief second, as I put it back in place, I thought the girls were going to ask me some more about it, or about my hearing impairment in general, and I was actually planning to tell them about my streamer, which was an electronic device I sometimes used to transmit signals straight from my iPhone or iPod to my hearing aids, thus eliminating the need for headphones or earbuds completely, but they seemed to have had the majority of their questions addressed and they seemed pretty content with the answers I'd provided, so things switched to another topic - Riley's future plans with Jason. And from that point forward, as far as I was concerned, the night was a complete blast.

Reading Lips

Our first game of the Leavenworth Invite was the next morning and it was at a nice park just outside of town, not too far from a small river. It was against a team called the Mercer Island Magic. The Magic was actually a pretty good team, with a lot of good players, and they were unforgettable because of their uniforms. They wore bright pink jerseys that had purple stars all over them. They were undoubtedly the ugliest, most obnoxious uniforms I had ever seen, and I winced every time I looked at them. Anyway, the game was a good one and we won 5-3, and it was noteworthy for two innings in particular: the third and the fifth. In the third, something happened I had never seen before. The Magic were batting, and they had one out, but it was a promising inning for them since they had runners on first and second. Riley made a pitch which ended up being a ball, so the batter tossed her bat down and started jogging to first base. In the meantime, the base runners started heading toward second and third. At the time, I was completely fooled since I hadn't been keeping track of balls and strikes so I thought it was ball four and was a routine walk. In reality, however, it was ball three, and as such was a trick play. The Magic were trying to confuse us and, in essence, steal second and third without us even knowing (they assumed we would just stand there and do nothing while they trotted nonchalantly to the bases). It was a bad idea, however, since Danielle, Olivia, and Erin, who were experienced, intelligent players, would never be tricked by something like that. Danielle whipped the ball to Olivia, who tagged the runner heading to third, then she threw the ball to Erin, who tagged the runner heading to second.

Just like that, the Magic's trickery was thwarted and the inning was over. Russell was so impressed with how Danielle, Olivia, and Erin had handled things he gave them hugs the minute they returned to the dugout.

"Well done, ladies. Well done, indeed."

Amazingly, however, that wasn't the end of the trickery. Russell decided that since the Magic had tried a trick play, we might as well try one, too. So in the fifth inning, when the Magic had a runner on third base and two outs, he sent Danielle a signal to attempt to pick her off. Danielle whipped the ball from home to third, but her throw was high and flew into the outfield. The runner, thinking she could score easily thanks to Danielle's errant throw, turned and ran for home. In reality, however, Danielle's throw hadn't been errant at all. She had purposefully thrown it over Olivia's head and straight to our left fielder, Kaitlin, who was standing there waiting for it. Kaitlin caught it, then fired it straight back to Danielle. The runner was out by a mile and we were cheering like there was no tomorrow.

I was completely amazed. I had never seen anything like it. My Little League teams had always been happy to just keep to the basics (and even the basics had been a challenge for us at times). But select girls loved trick plays and we were all smiles from that point forward. And Russell was so happy he offered to take us all out to ice cream afterward.

Our next game was against a team from Yakima called the Sidewinders. It wasn't as exciting as the first game and neither team tried any trick plays, but it was still fun and we won 6-3. We led the entire game and I got three hits including my first triple as a select player. It was a beauty of a shot, a line drive down the first base foul line. I ran as fast as I could and I was all of the way to second before the outfielder got to it and threw it back in. The shortstop caught it and tried to relay it to third in time to get me, but I slid under the tag easily.

As such, the day was spectacular, but things got even better when we returned to our hotel and headed for the pool. I had never been a big fan of pools, since I had to take my hearing aids out to go in (they weren't waterproof), but the rest of the girls were going and I didn't want to be left out, and it had been a really hot day so it sounded pretty refreshing to me.

So we all got our bathing suits and met at the pool, and I'll be honest I did a double take the minute I saw Danielle. She was wearing a skimpy, navy bikini, and let's just say she was much closer to becoming the woman she would be than the girl she had been. She had amazing hips, long legs, and a huge chest. I had heard from the other girls she was really popular with boys, and after seeing her in her bikini I knew why. I instantly got a little jealous and I desperately hoped I would look like her in another year or so.

Anyway, we all jumped into the pool and it was great fun. As expected, the water was cool and refreshing and we took turns tossing a beach ball from side to side. At one point, I had it in my hands and Erin called out to me to throw it to her, so I did. She caught it, then went to toss it to Riley, who was a few feet away in the pool's deep end, but stopped abruptly as she realized something.

"How did you do that?"

"Do what?"

"How did you hear me? I thought you said you had to take your hearing aids off before you got into the pool."

"I did. I put them in my bag over there. By that chair. I have a case just for them."

She raised an eyebrow. "But I thought you said you can't hear without them."

"I can't."

"So how can you hear me right now?"

"I can't."

"So how are you talking to me?"

Her eyes got big the second I answered.

"I'm reading your lips."

"You can do that? That's amazing. I've heard of that, but I didn't think it was possible."

"Me, neither," Riley said. She had walked up and was standing right next to Erin. "I thought lip reading was an urban myth."

"Not at all. It can be done, and for a while, especially when I was young, I had no choice. My first pair of hearing aids wasn't that good since the technology was pretty shaky back then, and they irritated my ears so I took them out a lot and when I did I had to have another way to communicate with my parents. So I learned how to read lips."

"How?" Riley asked. "Did you take lessons?"

I shook my head. "No. I just taught myself. I would watch people's lips carefully and it took quite a while, but eventually I learned how to do it. Over the years I've gotten better and better, but of course I'm not always perfect. I sometimes struggle if a person is speaking too quickly or isn't enunciating their words properly. And men with mustaches are really tough since their mustaches usually cover parts of their lips."

"That's incredible," Danielle said. At that point, she had overheard our conversation and had joined in. "Can all people who have hearing impairments read lips?"

I shook my head. "I don't think so. Not as well as me, at least."

"I've got to see this in action," Erin said. She looked across the pool and pointed at a man sitting in a patio chair. He was wearing a red tank top and was talking to a woman who was sitting in the chair next to him. "Read his lips."

I looked right at him, then, like I always did when I was attempting to read someone's lips, I concentrated as hard as I could. Much to my delight, he spoke clearly and succinctly so his words were immediately visible to me. I caught everything he said easily.

"He's asking her where she wants to go for dinner. He wants to know if pizza sounds good."

The other girls cracked up the minute I said it. Erin could barely contain her excitement.

"That's amazing. From this distance, I can't hear a thing he's saying. I've never seen anything like it, Melody. Try someone else. Try that girl over there."

I looked to the man's left, to a couple of girls who were sitting on a small bench next to a tree. They looked like they were in their early teens and probably were just a year or two younger than I was. Like most girls their age, they were texting on their phones while they spoke to one another. One of the girls was a little tough to read since she mashed her lips together as she spoke, but I caught almost everything she said anyway.

"The girl in the red wants to know what the other girl thinks of a boy named Bobby Sullivan."

At that, the other girl, who had a long ponytail and was dressed primarily in blue, made a funny face.

"Bobby Sullivan?" I said, repeating her words as she spoke. "He's gross. Don't tell me you like him." I turned back to the other girl, the one in the red. "Maybe."

At that, Erin, Riley, and Danielle could barely contain their excitement. None of them had ever seen anything like it, and Riley signaled for the rest of the team to come over and check it out.

"You've got to see this. Melody is like a superhero, with this crazy super ability. She can read people's lips from far away."

At that, I did it again, this time so the rest of the team could see.

"The girl in blue says she likes a boy named Chad Fulcher. The girl in red says she thinks he's really cute."

The rest of the team had the same response Erin, Riley, and Danielle had had. Their eyes lit up the minute I did it.

"You've got to do it on me," Kaitlin said. "I'm going to run over there near the bathrooms, and you tell the other girls what I'm saying."

Barely able to contain her excitement, she climbed out of the pool and ran over to a small, brick building that was about as far away from me as she could get while still being visible. From there, she was way out of earshot, even for people who have excellent hearing and don't need hearing aids. She looked right at me and her lips started to move.

I giggled the minute I saw her words.

"What?" Riley asked. "What's she saying?"

"She says I'm amazing. But she says you're a spoiled brat. And she thinks your mama dresses you funny."

Everyone laughed. Despite the comment, Riley wasn't offended at all since she knew Kaitlin was just kidding, and instead she was focused on my 'ability' as she called it.

At that, Kaitlin ran back over to us, and, just to see how I had done, Riley asked her to tell us exactly what she had said.

"I said Melody is amazing but you're a spoiled brat and your mama dresses you funny."

The girls cheered the minute they realized I had read her lips word-for-word.

Kaitlin's eyes got big as she saw their response. "She did it? Perfectly? That's incredible."

I spent the rest of the night entertaining them. I took turns reading each of their lips from afar. Each of them ran to a spot somewhere out of earshot then gave it a try. Eventually, news of my 'special ability' even made it to Russell, who was sunbathing in an inflatable, floating chair on the far side of the pool.

"That could be pretty useful some day, Melody. Maybe when you get older you should look into becoming a secret agent or something like that. I imagine the FBI or the CIA could use someone with an ability like that."

To be honest, I didn't really know what to think about his comment. Like most fourteen-year-old girls, I hadn't really thought too much about my future, nor what I wanted to be when I got older, but a secret agent did sound pretty cool. Maybe I'd get a fancy car and some neat gadgets, like a tube of lipstick that was actually a miniature bomb in disguise, and maybe I'd get to travel all around the world to exotic places like Rio de Janeiro and Barcelona, and I'd get to battle evil villains who were intent on destroying the world.

It sounded pretty cool, there was no doubt about that, but to be honest at the time I was pretty content just to be a softball player, on a team like the Skyhawks, and I was absolutely loving all of the attention I was getting. Unfortunately, however, the sun finally went down and we had to round up our stuff and leave the pool, but that's when something new and even more exciting happened.

I met a boy.

A really cute one.

Steven

It didn't actually happen until later that night. After leaving the pool, we went up to our rooms, took showers, then went out for a while. Russell and the rest of the dads, including mine, were fine with it as long as we stayed together, checked in once an hour, and didn't go too far from the hotel. We spent the first hour or so wandering around the downtown area, looking at the various sites, including a small park that was filled with artists showing their paintings, then we found a store called The Candy Shoppe that sold old-fashioned taffy. It was made right there in the store's lobby, in a machine that stretched and twisted it right in front of us. I got a bag and it was so good my taste buds went wild the minute I put a piece in my mouth. After The Candy Shoppe, we went to a miniature golf course, rented some clubs, and played a round. Nobody in the group knew how to keep score, since none of us were golf fans, so we just played for the fun of it and had a great time. Everyone cheered as I made a hole-in-one on the ninth hole, which was surprising since it was one of the more difficult holes and gave some of the other girls complete fits. Riley hit her ball into a pool of water, and she had to take her shoes and socks off and wade in in order to get it back. Anyway, the real excitement, however, didn't begin until we finished our round of golf and went into the clubhouse to return our clubs. At the time, it was really busy, and it was filled with kids and teenagers, and a group of teenage boys instantly caught Erin's eye. There were four of them and they were hanging out on the far side of the room near a row of arcade games. Two of them were busy playing a game that looked like some type of motorcycle simulator. It even had seats and handlebars that looked like real motorcycles.

"I saw them out on the course while we were playing," Erin said. "They were a few holes ahead of us but I had a feeling they would wait around until we finished."

"Why do you say that?" Danielle asked.

Erin smiled, then pointed at one of them. He was tall and muscular, with broad shoulders and a thick neck. Clearly, a football player, and probably a lineman. "That one has his eye on you."

Danielle smiled. She clearly liked the fact a guy was checking her out. Especially a tall, muscular football player.

"Nice," she said.

Erin pointed at a second boy. This one wasn't nearly as big as the first, and he looked like he was a year or two younger, but as far as I was concerned he was absolutely dreamy. He had short, dark hair, dimples on both cheeks, and the nicest smile I had ever seen.

"That one has his eye on Melody."

My heart skipped a beat the minute she said it.

"What?"

Erin nodded. "He's been checking you out since the fifth hole. I've seen him look your way at least three different times. He was clearly impressed when you got that hole-in-one."

At that, Kaitlin overhead our conversation and joined in. "You should go over and talk to him, Melody."

I instantly got hesitant. "I don't know about that."

"Why not? Do you have a boyfriend?"

"No. I don't."

"Then why not head over and say hi? He's really cute. Trust me, if he was checking me out, I'd be over there in a flash."

"I'm not really comfortable doing things like that."

Danielle raised an eyebrow. "Why not? Don't you like boys?"

"I like boys. Especially that one. He's really cute. But they don't like me."

All three girls looked at me with puzzled expressions on their faces.

"What?" they asked, in unison.

"Boys don't want a girlfriend who is deaf. They want a girl who can hear like the rest of you."

Danielle's answer was immediate and straight-to-the-point. "That's the dumbest thing I've ever heard, Melody."

"I agree," Erin said. "We girls don't care about your hearing impairment, so why would those boys care about it?"

"Boys are different than girls. They think and act a lot differently than us."

Danielle thought about it for a while, then nodded. "Ok. I won't argue with you there. They are different, but I still don't think they care about something like a hearing impairment. Has something happened to you in the past to lead you to think otherwise?"

Somewhat hesitantly, I told them about the only date I had ever been on. It had happened the year before, when I had gone to dinner with a boy named Caleb Hightower. I had had a great time and had wanted to go out with him again, but apparently he had felt otherwise since he had never asked me out again.

"That's it?" Erin asked. "You had one date that didn't work out and you're ready to give up on boys completely? That's silly."

"On your date," Danielle asked, "did Caleb say anything about your hearing impairment?"

"No. I don't recall him mentioning it at all."

"So why do you think he was turned off by it?"

"What else could it have been? What else could have made him not want to go out with me again?"

Danielle laughed. "It could have been anything. Do you know how many dates I've been on that went absolutely nowhere? Too many to remember. I think you're reading too much into it, Melody. I don't think your bad experience with Caleb had anything to do with your hearing impairment. I think it just wasn't meant to be."

"Me, too," Erin said.

"Me, three," Kaitlin said.

I didn't really know what to think. Deep down, I wanted to believe them, and I felt like I could since they were all older than me and knew a lot more about boys than I did, but at the same time I was still reluctant. I had really liked Caleb, and when things hadn't worked out with him it had really disappointed me and hurt my feelings. As such, I didn't want to risk going through that type of heartache again.

At the same time, however, I couldn't help but shoot another glance across the room at the boy. He was so cute. I didn't think I had ever seen a boy as cute as him before.

"I've got an idea," Erin said. She turned to me. "Melody, tell me what that boy, the big one who likes Danielle, is saying. Read his lips for me."

I did what she said. I concentrated on the boy she had referred to, the muscular one, who was talking to another boy who was standing next to him and wearing a baseball cap. I repeated his words aloud as he said them. "I'm thinking about going over to talk to her. What do you think? Should I do it, or should I just wait and see if she'll come over here?"

The boy with the baseball cap responded, so I read his lips. "I think you should play it cool for a while and see if she'll come over here."

Erin was all smiles as she listened to me. Clearly, her plan, whatever it was, was developing as intended, but there was one more part to it.

"Now switch your attention to the boy who likes you. Tell us what he's saying right now."

Once again, I did as told, and I focused on the boy who (allegedly) liked me. He was talking to the fourth boy, who was wearing a gray T-shirt and blue jeans. The boy in the gray T-shirt spoke first. "Come on, man, you can do it. Just have a little faith. She'll like you."

The boy who (allegedly) liked me responded. "I'm not like the rest of you, I'm not as outgoing. Especially around girls. It's hard for me to just walk up to them and start talking."

"But she's cute, Steven. Don't waste the chance. You like her, right?"

He didn't even think about it. His answer was immediate and it froze me in my tracks. I was so stunned I didn't even say it aloud.

The other girls went crazy.

"What'd he say?" Danielle asked.

"Tell us," Erin said.

"Right now," Kaitlin said.

My eyes were huge and my heart was absolutely racing as I told them what he had said. "He said he does. A lot."

Suddenly, my attitude had changed completely. Now that I knew for certain he liked me, I really did want to meet him, but I didn't know how.

"What do you think I should do?"

"Go over and talk to him," Erin said.

I shook my head. "I can't do that. I'm too nervous. I wouldn't even make it halfway across the room before I'd chicken out."

"Well then just walk over by him and hang out for a while. Don't go up to him, just meander around in the general area."

"What will that do?"

"It'll give him a chance to wander over and talk to you. If you can't say hi to him maybe he'll say hi to you."

It made some sense to me but I was still uncomfortable and hesitant. Luckily, Danielle took over and came to my aid.

"I have a better plan. Come with me and follow my lead."

She started to walk toward the group of boys but stopped abruptly as she noticed I wasn't following her. Instead, I was just standing there, frozen in place with a stupid look on my face. I had never done anything like that before and I was terrified.

Danielle shot me a stern glance. "Remember yesterday, at dinner, when you said you wanted to be treated like a normal person? And you said you didn't want to be treated any differently because of your hearing impairment? Well now

I'm going to do what you wanted and treat you like any other girl, and Kaitlin and Erin are going to help me. We're going to put as much peer pressure on you as it takes to get you to come with me and talk to that boy."

At first, I was in complete shock, and I had no idea what to do since I had never been in a situation like that before and was clearly out of my element, but any decision I had to make was made not by me, but instead by Erin. She stepped behind me and said, "Here's my version of peer pressure." She then pushed me in the back and literally forced me to follow Danielle across the room. To someone watching from the outside it probably looked pretty funny -- one girl pushing another forcibly across the room. But at the same time it was effective and got the job done. Ever so reluctantly, I acquiesced and followed Danielle across the room.

All four boys turned to face us the minute we walked up. I stayed one step behind Danielle the whole time.

"Hi, guys. I'm Dani, and this is Melody, and we were wondering if we could hang with you for a while."

All four boys answered at once, in unison.

"Of course."

"Please do."

"Nice to meet you."

"That's great."

They then caught themselves and tried to look cool.

"I mean, yeah, that's fine," the football player said.

The four of them introduced themselves. The football player was Tyler, the boy in the baseball cap was Peter, the boy in the gray T-shirt was Wyatt, and the boy who liked me was Steven.

"Are you guys from around here?" Danielle asked. "Do you go to a school here in Leavenworth?"

"No," Tyler said. "We're actually from Everett."

My eyes got big the minute he said it. Everett was a small city about twenty minutes north of Seattle, and it was less than ten minutes away from my home in Mill Creek.

"Everett?" Danielle asked. "What brings you all of the way to Leavenworth?"

"We came over to have some fun and to get away from Everett for a while. There's not a whole lot to do there other than the movie theater. And Steven was coming anyway, since his sister plays softball and is here for the tournament."

Danielle turned to Steven. "Who's your sister?"

"Paige. Paige Parker."

Danielle's eyes got big the minute he said the name. "Paige Parker? The same Paige Parker who plays for the Missfits?"

Steven nodded. "Yeah, that's her. Do you know her?"

"Uh, yeah. Everyone who plays softball knows her. She's the best pitcher around. She struck me out like ten times last year. Probably more."

Everyone laughed. I couldn't really believe my luck. The potential boy of my dreams was from Everett, and he had an older sister who was a softball player. We hadn't even said anything to one another but already we had a couple of things in common.

"What about you?" the boy named Peter asked. "We saw the two of you with a group of girls earlier. Are you on a softball team?"

Danielle nodded. "We play for Skyhawks Fastpitch. I'm the catcher and Melody is our center fielder."

"Really?" Steven asked, and for the first time he looked right at me. For a second our eyes met and I thought I was going to pass out right there on the spot. My knees got weak and I started to sweat. "I'm the center fielder on my team at school. I go to Everett High."

Danielle turned to me and smiled. "Everett is near Jackson, isn't it, Melody?"

She was clearly trying to coax me into the conversation since I hadn't said a single thing yet, and to be honest I felt pretty dumb since I hadn't, but at the same time I hadn't really known what to say and I was worried about what would happen when the boys heard my voice for the first time. How would they react, especially Steven? Would it turn him off and scare him away?

Regardless, I decided I needed to do something, sooner rather than later, so I responded.

"It is."

Much to my relief, my voice didn't bother them at all, especially Steven, and he took a step closer and said, "You go to Jackson?"

"I do."

"I just played a game against them last week. They're awesome. Do you know any of the players on the team? Like Logan Smith? He's a good friend of mine."

I couldn't believe it. I knew Logan Smith. He was a boy in my math and English classes.

"I have some classes with him."

Danielle's eyes got big. "Wow. Look at how much the two of you have in common." She turned to the other boys. "Why don't you three come with me and meet the rest of my friends? In the meantime, these two can get to know each other a little better."

Much to my surprise, she turned and led the other boys away from us. They went to the far side of the room where the rest of the girls were monitoring our progress closely. They all looked away and pretended they were doing other things as soon as Danielle and the boys headed their way. Steven and I were left standing there, by ourselves, which was kind of nerve-racking at first, but much to my relief and delight thus began one of the best nights of my life. Steven and I hit it off right from the start, and we had so many things in common: favorite food (spaghetti with meatballs), zodiac sign (Libra), least favorite subjects in school (math and science), favorite football team (Seahawks), and, as he had mentioned before, we both played the same position (center field). Our only difference was our ages, since he was sixteen, but to me that was a good thing because I had always liked the idea of dating an older boy. For about twenty minutes we just stood there near the arcade games talking, but then he asked if I was thirsty and wanted a drink and he bought me a Sprite, and as we were standing in line to get it I snuck a quick peek across the room and saw Erin and Riley monitoring us closely, and they both gave me a thumbs up. I was still a little nervous, since I wasn't used to dealing with boys, but at the same time I couldn't believe how well things were going. But then something unexpected happened. Just after we got our drinks Steven surprised me by asking me about my hearing impairment.

"Do you mind if I ask? I noticed you're wearing hearing aids. Do you have something wrong with your hearing?"

I instantly got apprehensive. "I do. Does that bother you?"

"No. Not at all. I was just wondering. And I apologize if I made you uncomfortable by mentioning it."

There was real concern in his eyes, and I could tell he was worried he had screwed things up between us. As far as I was concerned, however, he hadn't, not in the least, so I quickly came to his aid.

"It's okay. I have a severe hearing impairment, and I've had it since I was four. That's why my voice sounds funny."

A puzzled looked formed on his face. "I don't think your voice sounds funny at all. I can understand you no problem. And I hope I'm not being too forward, since we just met, but talking to you has been the highlight of my weekend."

Highlight of the weekend? As far as I was concerned, talking to him had been the highlight of my life. And speaking of talking, we continued to do it for the rest of the night, and we would have probably continued talking forever, but finally Erin came over and interrupted us.

"Russell just called and he wants us to head back to the hotel soon. He doesn't want us to stay out too late since we have a game first thing in the morning."

My eyes got big as I looked at my phone and saw it was almost 10:00 pm. I couldn't believe it. I had been talking to Steven for almost two hours straight, yet to me it had only seemed like fifteen minutes. As such, we exchanged phone numbers, then said goodbye, and he totally made my day by saying, "I'm going to be at the fields tomorrow to watch some of Paige's games. I'll come by and watch one of yours if it's okay."

A boy, coming to watch me play a game? It was more than okay. It was like I had died and gone to heaven.

On the way back to our hotel, every girl on the team patted me on the back and of course they teased me a little, and at one point Erin said, "That's pretty impressive, Melody. It's your first road trip with the team and already you picked up a boy. Even Danielle can't make that claim. On her first road trip she never talked to anyone. She was too timid and shy back then."

Everyone laughed, and we arrived at our hotel a few minutes later and I got ready and went to bed, but I didn't get much sleep that night. I was so excited I could hardly hold still and I kept tossing and turning under my covers, and you can probably guess who I was thinking about the whole time.

Texts from Boys

The next day, I was tired, since I had gotten so little sleep the night before, but at the same time I was excited and raring to go, and I couldn't wait to get to the fields to get the day's games underway. Weekend tournaments were a lot different than Summer League, and on Sundays during weekend tournaments you only got to keep playing until you lost a game, and once you did, you were done and your tournament was over. But if you somehow managed to win all of your games, you got a shiny trophy and a championship T-shirt. But I wasn't excited about a shiny trophy and a championship T-shirt. I was excited about Steven. I couldn't wait to see him again and when I did, I was going to go out of my way to impress him.

During warmups, the other girls couldn't help but tease me a little.

"So," Erin said. "Any word from your beau yet?"

The other girls laughed the minute she said the word 'beau.'

"Not yet."

"The rest of us have already placed bets. We're all betting on when he's going to text you for the first time. I've got five bucks on the first inning."

I laughed. I could hardly believe what I had just heard. The girls were making bets on when Steven was going to text me? That was hilarious.

But then something occurred to me.

"He already said he was coming. Why would he text me?"

"That's what boys do. They text you. Especially when they like you. And he clearly does. I was watching him last night while he was talking to you and I could see it in his eyes."

"What do you mean?"

"His eyes sparkled every time he looked at you. Surely you could feel it."

"What do you mean?"

"When he looked at you, into your eyes, how did you feel?"

"Like I was going to melt."

"Exactly. The two of you have amazing chemistry, especially for a couple who just met."

At that, Danielle, who was listening to our conversation but hadn't said anything yet, couldn't help but chime in.

"If you look up the word chemistry in a dictionary you'll see a photo of Melody and Steven right next to it."

Everyone laughed. Including me.

"You wait and see," Erin said. "He's going to text you this morning. It's just a matter of when."

"What will he say?"

"Hard to say. Probably nothing important, but that's irrelevant. The only thing that matters is that he did. And if he does it during the first inning, it'll be perfect because then I'll win the bet."

Warmups continued from there and I was even more excited than before, which was hard to believe since I was already so excited I could barely control myself. Having Steven come to a game was still my main focus, but I really liked the idea of him texting me, too, so as soon as we finished our warmups I darted to the dugout, dug my phone out of my softball bag where I normally kept it, and checked it.

It should be noted I wasn't really allowed to do that. We girls weren't allowed to text or make phone calls during games, and technically we weren't even supposed to have our phones in the dugout at all. But on that particular day, I had no choice. I had to know if he had sent me a text or not.

And the other girls had to know, too. They saw me checking my phone and waited anxiously for my report. Some of them stood in front of me so Russell and the other coaches couldn't see what I was doing.

Unfortunately, my screen was blank.

"That's okay," Danielle said. "Actually, it's perfect. If he holds off until the third inning I win the bet."

The game started a few minutes later and it was against a team from Idaho called the Stampede. They wore red and black uniforms and were quite good, but they weren't my focus, not at all. Every inning, as soon as we got the final out, I darted from my spot in center field and went straight for my phone. For the first three innings its screen remained blank and I was pretty disappointed, but then, when I grabbed it during the fourth inning, my eyes lit up and my heart raced.

There was a message.

"Hi. It's me, Steven. Just wanted to see how you're doing."

The entire team cheered the minute I made the announcement. Kaitlin cheered the loudest since she had won the bet. Russell looked over, to see what all of the commotion was about, and we all pretended to be doing nothing so he returned to his coaching duties.

But then a question came to mind. I had finally received the long-awaited text, but now what was I supposed to do in response?

The answer was obvious to Erin. "Text him back."

"What should I say?"

"Anything. Just be yourself."

"But I've never texted a boy before. What if I say something stupid?"

"Just keep it simple. Tell him about the game."

I was still a little nervous but telling him about the game didn't seem too difficult, and I didn't see how I could mess that up so I grabbed my phone and started typing.

"We're playing the Stampede. It's 0-0 in the fourth."

"Sweet," he wrote back. "I'm watching my sister's game. They're playing the Bellevue Beast. It's 0-0."

In the meantime, on the field, Danielle grounded into a force play to end the inning so I had to put my phone back into my bag and return to the field. But as soon as we got three outs I was back in a flash. And thus began my routine for the rest of the game. I would send Steven texts every inning, while I was in the dugout, and he would text back. It went something like this:

"It's still 0-0," I wrote. "We got them 1, 2, 3. Riley struck out 2 of the batters. She's really sharp today. Actually, she's sharp every day."

"Sweet," Steven responded. "My sister, Paige, struck out 2 batters too. They're ahead 1-0 in the third."

"Sweet. Darn, the Stampede just turned a double play. Gotta go."

A few minutes later, I was back.

"We got them 1, 2, 3 again. I made a running catch to end the inning."

"Well done. I wish I could have seen it. Paige's team is leading 3-0. The shortstop hit a home run with two outs."

"Sweet. I gotta go. It's my turn to bat."

A few minutes later, I was back.

"I got a single, straight up the middle, then scored when Sophia hit a double. They tried to get me at home but I was safe by a mile."

"Sweet."

"We just scored again. Olivia hit a homer. We're ahead 4-0."

"Sweet."

"Gotta go. Kaitlin popped out to center."

A few minutes later, I was back. This time, a message was waiting for me upon my arrival.

"Paige just hit a grand slam. It's 7-0. The rout is on."

"Sweet. Your sister must be awesome."

"She thinks so. Haha. Actually, she is. But then again, she should be since she practices so much. She's hardcore when it comes to softball. I bet you're the same."

"Sometimes. Sweet. Erin just hit a single and the bases are loaded. We're about to blow it open."

Sure enough, we did. Riley was the next batter and she hit a double down the left field line, scoring all three base runners, then Jamie followed with a double that scored Riley. The final score ended up being 8-0 and everyone was happy because the victory meant we got to continue the tournament and play another game. I was the happiest of all, because a few minutes later I got the following text:

"Paige's game just ended. It was 9-0. The guys and I are heading your way. See you soon."

I could barely wait.

Grand Slam

I had always loved playing softball, since it was such a fun game, but trust me, it was even better when a cute boy like Steven was watching me. I was a little nervous, of course, because I wanted to do well and impress him, but luckily my nervousness was suppressed by my excitement. I still couldn't believe what had happened. I had met a boy, a really nice one, and he was sitting right there in the stands, just a few feet away, cheering for me. I felt like I was the queen of the world.

And I played like it. Our game was against a team from Oregon called the Pioneers and I made two catches in the first inning, one in the second, and another in the third. I got my first at-bat later that same inning and I was so excited I hit the very first pitch that was thrown to me, even though it was low and away and I probably shouldn't have swung at it at all. Anyway, much to my relief and delight it raced past the Pioneers' shortstop for a single. I grounded out in the fifth, but I didn't let that bother me too much. Things didn't get really interesting, however, until the bottom of the seventh. The score was 2-2 but the Pioneers handed us a golden opportunity when their shortstop made a throwing error and the bases ended up loaded as a result. As such, if we could get a hit, even something as weak as a bloop single, the runner on third would score and we would win.

And guess who the next batter was?

You guessed it. It was me.

It was like a dream come true. I had the chance to win the game, in the bottom of the final inning, with Steven sitting right there watching me. I couldn't get from the on-deck circle to the batter's box fast enough. Everyone was cheering and chanting my name as I dug my cleats into the dirt, then tapped my bat on the far edge of the plate, measuring my distance from it carefully. As soon as I was set, I turned and faced the pitcher, who was a short, thin girl with a nose that looked much too big for her face. Her first pitch was down in the dirt for a ball, as was the one after that, but her third was on the outside corner for a strike. For a second I contemplated swinging at it, but since I was ahead in the count I knew I should be patient and wait for something better. And I was glad I did. The next pitch came straight down the middle of the plate. I was so excited I nearly jumped out of my socks the minute I saw it coming. I swung my bat as hard as I could, then stood there in complete shock as the ball raced toward the outfield fence. The Pioneers' center fielder never even tried to catch it. She just stood there and watched as it soared into the distance.

I couldn't believe it. I would have been happy with a single, since that would have won the game for us, but a grand slam? I had never hit a grand slam in my entire life, not even in Little League.   My teammates raced from the dugout, and as soon as I circled the bases and got back to home plate, they tackled me and jumped on top of me in a classic pigpile. As we finally calmed down and started to get up and head back to our dugout, Danielle took a quick glance at Steven, who was still cheering loudly from his place in the stands, then turned to me and said, "If that doesn't impress him, nothing will."

Paige

Unfortunately for us, however, the fun, and our tournament, ended the very next game. Of all the teams we could face, our next opponent was Steven's sister's team, Missfits Fastpitch, and they were incredible. Especially Steven's sister, Paige. She was a tall, pretty girl with deep auburn hair and hazel eyes, and she was undoubtedly the best pitcher I had ever seen. She made Riley look mediocre by comparison, which was amazing since Riley was a great pitcher. Her pitches were so fast they looked like bright, yellow streaks as they came at me. She struck out eight of our first nine batters, including me. I fouled off one of her pitches, but that was the best I could do.

"Nice try, Melody," Steven shouted from the stands. "You'll get the next one."

But then his eyes got big as he realized Paige was standing in the pitching circle, looking straight at him. The look on her face was priceless, and it was more than clear she wasn't happy her brother was cheering for the opposing team.

Quickly, he tried to save face. "Nice pitch, Paige. Bring the heat, sis."

Everyone started to laugh, and we all realized he was in a strange, no-win situation. He had to cheer for both teams at the same time.

The game continued from there and it was pretty much more of the same. We finally managed to get a couple of hits off of Paige, but they were few and far between. In the meantime, the Missfits scored four runs, two in the fifth and two in the sixth, and they ended up winning 4-0. We were all pretty disappointed to lose since it meant our time in Leavenworth was finally at an end, but something interesting happened as soon as the game concluded. Like usual, we lined up and shook the other team's hands, one by one, but everything came to a temporary halt as I got to Paige. The minute she saw me, she smiled and said, "So you're the reason my brother is in such a good mood today. It's nice to meet you, Melody."

I don't know if I was star-struck, since Paige was an older player and was so good, or if I was just nervous because she was Steven's older sister, or maybe it was a combination of both, but I basically just stood there in front of her, wide-eyed and silent. Erin, who was in line right behind me, had to bump me in the back to snap me out of it and get me to say something.

"It's nice to meet you."

I would have liked to have said something a little more original, and maybe something a little more articulate, but at the time "It's nice to meet you" was the only thing I could think of.

"Hopefully I'll see you again," Paige said. "Hopefully soon."

"That would be nice," I said.

She smiled, then moved on and started shaking hands with the other girls.

At that, our tournament was officially over, so we rounded up our stuff, placed it in our cars, and prepared to head for home.

But there was one more thing that happened before we left Leavenworth. Right before I got in the car to head home (my dad was talking with Russell at the time), Steven walked up and said, "I was wondering. If you have some free time this week, maybe you'd like to go out. It doesn't have to be anything fancy. Maybe just coffee or –"

I didn't even let him finish.

"I'd love to."

I was nothing but smiles the whole drive home.

Fun with Riley

Our next Summer League game was against a team called the Washington LadyCats. Undoubtedly, they were one of the best teams we played that year, and they were almost as good as the Missfits. As was customary, Russell gave us a pep talk and scouting report during warmups and he warned us about one player in particular.

"We need to be really careful with their shortstop. Her name is Kiana. Kiana Cruise. She's originally from Anaheim and like a lot of California girls she's really good. If possible, don't hit anything at her or you're pretty much as good as gone. She's stellar on defense."

I couldn't help but smile. I didn't know her, since she was three years older than I was, but I had heard the name before since she was a fellow classmate of mine at Jackson. She was a lean, athletic girl with curly, black hair, and she was every bit as good as Russell had told us, if not better. She roamed the infield like she owned the place and nothing, no matter how hard it was hit, no matter where it was hit, got past her. In the first inning, Erin hit a nice shot straight up the middle which would have been a single for sure against any other shortstop, but Kiana made an incredible running play and threw her out by a step. Two batters later, Kaitlin hit one over Kiana's head into shallow left center, but Kiana dropped back and made a diving catch. I had never seen anyone who could get to a ball like that before. Her range was incredible.

Amazingly, however, Kiana wasn't our biggest problem that day. Our biggest problem was one of our own players. Riley showed up for the game and it was clear from the start she was in a bad mood. Apparently, she and Jason had gone out again, the night before, but things hadn't gone nearly as well as their first date. I never got the specifics, but apparently at one point while they were eating, she caught him looking at another girl who was sitting at a nearby table. Riley described her as a "trampy blonde wearing a skimpy top." As such, Riley was distracted and aloof for much of the game, and we could tell she just didn't want to be there. Her pitches weren't nearly as fast as normal and she was missing her spots badly, which was unusual since she was usually so precise with her aim. She walked two batters in the first inning, two in the second, and one in the third. Luckily, we were able to get out of each inning without allowing any runs but only because our defense was rock solid. Our middle infielders (Erin and Jamie) turned a double play to end the first, and Olivia made a great running catch to end the second. Regardless, we knew things weren't going to bode well for us for long, since you can't beat a team as good as the

LadyCats unless you're firing on all cylinders. Russell could see the problem, too, and after the end of the third inning he had Megan start to warm up and it was clear he was planning to make a pitching change the next inning.

Which to me sounded like a good idea.

But not to Erin. She had another idea. She came up to me in the dugout between innings and said, "It's time we use that special ability of yours once again, Melody. Follow my lead and play along."

"What do you mean?"

"Just do what I do."

She turned and looked at Riley, who was sitting at the far end of the dugout with a distant look on her face. She was staring straight ahead and was clearly lost in her thoughts. In a voice that was just loud enough for her to hear, Erin said, "What's that, Melody? Those girls are talking about Riley? What'd they say?"

She looked back at me. I still didn't know what she was doing, so I just stood there with a confused look on my face. Luckily, however, she came to my aid and continued.

"You say they're badmouthing Riley?"

At that, Riley had clearly overheard her, since she turned and looked straight at us. At first she looked somewhat indifferent, but not for long. She stood up and walked down the dugout toward us.

"What's going on?"

Erin answered her question immediately. "Melody just told me she read the lips of that girl over there, the LadyCats' third baseman, and the girl said she can tell you're tired. And she said she's heard from other girls that once you get tired you're pretty much worthless. She thinks they can finish you off next inning but she's hoping Russell doesn't take you out before then so she can get another chance at you."

Riley's eyes narrowed. As I've mentioned before, she was a fiery, spirited girl, and normally she took great pride in her abilities, especially her pitching. As such, she was clearly offended by what Erin had said. She turned to me for verification. "Is that true? What are they saying now?"

For a second my eyes got big, but luckily I didn't give anything away. I had finally figured out what Erin was up to. She was trying to fire Riley up and get her back in the game so she could continue pitching and help us win. After all, she's our number one pitcher for a reason. I normally didn't like to lie to people, or even to tell half-truths, but in this case I had no choice since I didn't want to let Erin and the rest of the team down, so I decided to play along. I looked at the third baseman, who was standing on the field near Kiana. They were actually talking about Kiana's boyfriend, and the third baseman said, "He's so cute. I'd kill to have a boyfriend like that, Kiana." But what I told Riley she said was, "I haven't hit a home run all year, but since that pitcher is tired, I think I can get one off of her next inning. And it should be pretty easy since she's not throwing any heat today."

Riley's eyes got big. She was clearly offended by what I had said. "Really? She wants some heat? I'll give her some heat."

She spun on her heel and walked away. The minute she was out of earshot, Erin patted me on the back and said, "Well done, Melody."

I actually felt a little bad about it, about deceiving a teammate like that, but it worked to perfection. Riley went up to Russell and talked him into allowing her to stay in the game, for at least one more inning, and from that point forward she was her normal, feisty self. She threw nothing but heat and it was completely nasty. The LadyCats' batters (even Kiana) were overwhelmed. At one point, Riley struck out three of them in a row, and over a span of two innings she struck out five of six. The only batter who didn't strike out hit a weak grounder to Kaylee at first for an easy out. Kaylee hardly even had to move to make the play. So we were all smiles, as we had taken a 3-0 lead (Kaitlin and I hit singles, and Erin hit a home run to score all three of us), but things got even better the next inning when Riley struck out the LadyCats' third baseman, then turned to their dugout and shouted, "How do you like that? Does it look like I'm tired now?" None of them answered and they all had puzzled looks on their faces since they had no idea what she was talking about, but we

Skyhawks were completely cracking up. Word had spread around what Erin and I had done, and everyone thought it was hilarious. Even Russell was impressed, and he patted us both on the back and told us we would both be awarded game balls at the end of the game (which was a big deal to me since it was the first game ball I had ever been awarded as a select player).

We ended up winning 4-0, and at the end of the game, right after we did our post-game handshake with the LadyCats, Erin confessed and told Riley what we had done. At first I was worried Riley would be mad since we had tricked her, but in actuality I had nothing to worry about and she wasn't upset at all. Quite to the contrary, she laughed and said, "I should have known, Erin. You've always been a sly one."

She rounded up her stuff, put it in her bag, and started to leave. As she walked past me on her way out of the dugout, she paused just long enough to turn to me and say, "Well done, kid," then continued on her way.

Date Night

The next day was a big one for me. It was my date with Steven. The minute school let out for the day, I hurried home and spent the rest of the afternoon getting ready. I spent an hour in the bathroom getting my makeup just right (I went a little heavy on eye shadow, but I liked it anyway), then spent another hour working on my hair. I was having a bad hair day so it took quite a bit of effort on my part, but I finally got it just right and I arranged it in a way so it would cover my hearing aids completely. I knew I didn't really need to do that since Steven had already seen them and knew I wore them, but at the same time I was determined to look as good as possible for him. After finishing my makeup and hair, I went back into my bedroom and tried on ten different outfits, including multiple combinations of each, and I wasn't really happy with any of them so I finally just chose the tightest one I had. Unfortunately, that choice only lasted until I went downstairs to get something to drink and my dad saw me. He pointed at the staircase that led up to my room and said, "You're not wearing that."

I wasn't too happy since it had taken me so long to make my final decision, but at the same time I knew it wouldn't do any good to argue with him since he was really stubborn at times (and when I say 'at times' I mean all of the time). In addition, I didn't want to get in a fight with him and risk upsetting him, since he, like most dads who have teenage daughters, had insisted on meeting Steven before he would let me go out with him.

Steven arrived about twenty minutes later and he looked stunning. He was wearing a really nice pair of blue jeans and a fancy shirt, with a collar, and he clearly had put a little more gel in his hair than normal. I introduced him to my dad and we went into the living room for a while so we could talk and it went really well. At first, I thought my dad was going to interrogate him and try to make him feel uncomfortable, and maybe tell him a story involving a shotgun like most dads do, but he didn't, and he was actually cool the whole time. He loved the fact Steven was a baseball player since he, too, had been a baseball player back in his day (my dad had been a shortstop), and he also loved the fact Steven had an older sister (Paige) who played softball. We talked for about thirty minutes, then he stood up, shook Steven's hand and said, "Have a good time tonight. But since it's a weekday, make certain you're back by nine."

"Yes, sir," Steven said.

My dad smiled. "You can call me Dave."

At that, we were off. Steven was driving a white Toyota Corolla and it was actually his mom's car (since he had just gotten his license a few months before, he didn't have a car of his own yet). He took me to a restaurant in downtown Mill Creek called Pita Power, which served Mediterranean food, which was one of my favorites. For an appetizer, we got a plate of dolmas (grapevine leaves stuffed with rice and vegetables), then we had a Greek salad with cucumbers, kalamata olives, and feta cheese, then shared a gyro platter, then finished with some baklava, which was, in my opinion, the greatest dessert in the world. The food was great and I loved it, but it wasn't my focus. As you can probably guess, my focus was Steven.

For the first twenty minutes, it was pretty much just small talk and nothing all that noteworthy, but things really livened up once we started talking about his sister.

"That must be so cool," I said. "Having a sister. I've always wanted one."

"It has its moments. We only have one bathroom so I've spent plenty of time pounding on the door over the years."

I laughed.

"And she can be pretty tough at times. She's always been really headstrong and she never hesitates to remind me who's the boss. Once, when we were younger, she gave me a black eye."

I couldn't believe what I had just heard. Paige had given her own brother a black eye?

"It's true," he said. "But to be honest, it was partly my own fault. I was purposefully trying to irritate her —"

I couldn't help but interrupt.

"Wait a minute. You were trying to irritate her? Why would you do that?"

"That's what brothers do. Irritating our sisters is our job. Anyway, I had one of those rubber bats, the ones you blow up with your mouth, and I was poking her with it. She put up with it for about five minutes but then, without any warning whatsoever, she snatched it from me and clubbed me right across the face with it. I had a black eye for a week after that and it swelled up so bad I couldn't see out of it at all for the first couple of days."

I couldn't help but laugh. He should have known better. Poking a softball player, especially one as good as Paige, with an inflatable bat? That had trouble written all over it.

"A similar incident happened a few years later," he continued. "We were at the dinner table, eating, and I started putting a pot sticker in her face. I had it on my fork. I thought I was being pretty funny but not for long. She slapped it completely out of my hand. It flew all of the way across the room and splattered against the wall. My mom got so mad she made me spend the next half hour cleaning it up."

"That's great. Paige sounds like a tough cookie."

He nodded. "She is. But sometimes it actually comes in handy. Like back when I was in second grade. It was the first day of school and two older boys were picking on me. Paige came along, beat up one of them and chased the other one away. It was great. I never got picked on again 'cause nobody ever wanted to take their chances with her."

"Do you have any other brothers or sisters?"

He shook his head. "Nope. Which is probably good. Paige is more than enough for me."

We laughed, then he told me a little more about him. "I'm originally from North Carolina, Charlotte to be exact, but my family moved here when I was really young. As such, I don't remember Charlotte at all."

Over the years, I had been to Florida and Georgia, on a couple of family vacations, but I had never been to North Carolina so I couldn't say anything about it.

"What about you?" he asked. "Have you been to any cool places? Does your family travel much?"

I smiled. My dad had always been a fan of traveling, so we had gone on several trips over the years.

"Los Angeles is fun. I love the beaches there. And San Diego, too. Have you been to San Diego?"

He shook his head.

"There's this one place called Seaport Village. It's right in downtown, on the water, and it has an old-fashioned wooden boardwalk and all kinds of restaurants and shops, and even an old-school carousel. It's one of my favorite places in the world. Whenever we go there my dad and I always buy a kite and fly it in the park near the water. It's so much fun."

Steven smiled. "That sounds nice. Maybe someday we'll be lucky and get to go there together."

My heart raced at the thought of it. To me, Seaport Village was a magical place, but having Steven there with me would make it even better. I started to fantasize about the two of us sitting together on a bench along the boardwalk, watching the sailboats as they made their way into and out of the nearby marina, with the sun setting over the water on the distant horizon.

I hate to admit it, but I actually got so into the fantasy I hardly realized Steven was speaking again.

"Are there any other places you like?"

Finally coming back to reality, I thought for a second, then said, "Whistler."

He smiled the minute I said it. "Yeah. Whistler is great."

"You've been there?"

"Several times. My family and I went for the first time in 2010, for the Olympics, and we liked it so much we've been going there every year since. The first few years, we just went up during the winter, to go skiing, but this past year we went up during the summer and that was fun, too. I went bungee jumping for the first time."

My eyes got big the minute he said it. "You went bungee jumping?"

He nodded.

"How was it?"

"A total rush. As you can probably imagine, I was pretty scared at first when I was waiting for my turn on the top of the bridge. To be honest, I nearly chickened out, but somehow I managed to go through with it and I was pretty much filled with adrenaline for the rest of the day."

I laughed.

"Have you tried it?" he asked.

"No. I thought about it once, but I'm not quite that adventurous. When I go to Whistler, I like to do things like skiing and snowboarding, and during the summer I like hiking. About the wildest thing I've ever done up there was ziplining."

He smiled. "I tried that, too. It was great."

From that point forward, we continued talking about this and that, and just like the first day we met, back in Leavenworth, time flew by. Before I knew it, and much to my chagrin, it was 8:30 pm so he insisted on taking me home. At first, I was a little concerned about why he was so anxious to end the date and take me back, but then he gave me an explanation that completely made my day.

"I want to see you again. So I can't risk angering your dad or he might not let me."

We planned our next date, for the following Friday, and he took me home.

The Devils

My team's next game was the one we had been waiting for all season. The battle against the Devils, the team that had offered Riley a spot but dumped her less than a week later. We were all fired up, especially Riley, and we couldn't wait to get things underway. The Devils were a good team and they wore green and blue uniforms, which I thought was odd since to me Devils should wear red and yellow uniforms, but anyway, it was a battle from the start. Riley pitched better than I've ever seen her pitch and she struck out three of the first five batters, but the Devils weren't willing to go down without a fight, not for a second. They scored a run in the third inning when their first baseman, who was a huge, power-hitting righty, launched a home run to left, then scored one more in the fourth when their shortstop and second baseman hit back-to-back doubles. In the meantime, we got a run in the fourth when Erin hit a home run, then added two more in the fifth when Riley hit one of her own (you had to see the smile on her face when she did it – it was huge). As such, we went into the bottom of the seventh inning with a one run lead and we were really happy because we knew if we could get three more outs, we would win and Riley would finally get her revenge. She was so excited she could barely control herself in the pitching circle. Unlike normal, she was wandering all around the field between pitches, and shouting commands to us in our spots in the field behind her, and it was more than clear she wanted the victory badly. Things got off to a great start when the first batter hit a soft grounder to Erin at short. Erin scooped it up and threw it to Kaylee for an easy out. The second batter hit a fly ball to Sophia in right. But then things got interesting. Knowing there was only one out to go, Riley got too excited and lost focus. As such, she walked the next batter. It only took four pitches and none of them were even close to being strikes. Russell called timeout and headed to the pitching circle in an attempt to settle her down but his efforts were fruitless because her next pitch was wild and Danielle wasn't able to dig it out of the dirt. It got past her and went all of the way to the backstop. By the time she hustled back and grabbed it, the runner on first had advanced to second.

Russell tried once again to calm things down, this time from the dugout. "That's okay. No harm done, Riley. Focus on the batter. Don't worry about the runner."

Riley took several deep breaths and clearly she was trying her best to calm back down, but there was no mistaking she was nervous. And she wasn't the only one. I was watching wide-eyed from my spot in center field and I could barely breathe. We were so close to victory I could taste it, but at the same time, the runner on second base was big trouble. If the next batter got a hit, even something as weak as a bloop single, the runner would likely score and the game would be tied.

Riley took her spot, then made the next pitch. It was a good one, right across the outer edge of the plate, so I was relieved but only for a second. The batter took a mighty swing and crushed it, right into the gap between me and Kaitlin in left. At first, I was heartbroken because I knew there was no way either of us could get to it in time to catch it, and as a result I thought the runner on second would score for sure. But as I got to it and fielded it on a hop, I realized something. There was still hope, albeit not much. The runner wasn't overly fast and she had just rounded third, so if I made the throw of a lifetime I might be able to nail her at home plate. As such, I wound up and threw the ball as hard as I could, and for a second I thought I had thrown my shoulder out in the process. Much to my delight, however, the throw was a great one, undoubtedly the best I had ever done, and it was right on target with no arc whatsoever. It got to Danielle right as the runner got there. She nabbed it out of the air and slapped the runner right as she slid into the plate.

A second later, my prayers were answered when the umpire stood straight up, raised his right hand into the air, and shouted, "Out!"

And then the party started. The minute Riley heard the umpire's call, she threw her mitt into the air, charged at Danielle, and tackled her right there on the spot. A second later, Erin and the rest of the infielders rushed from their spots and jumped on top of them, and the outfielders, me included, jumped on top of the infielders. It was so much fun I couldn't believe it. Our parents grabbed their cameras and phones and started taking photos, and my dad got some really good ones. In one of them I was completely upside down and two other girls, Kaylee and Olivia, were right on top of me. In another, I was flat on my back with Danielle's foot in my face. My favorite, however, was the one my dad took a few minutes later, after we had all climbed back to our feet, and it was one of Riley with her arms around me, hugging me tightly. Right after my dad took the photo, Riley turned to me and said, "That was the best throw I've ever seen, kid. I don't know how you did it, but I owe you big time."

Date Number Two

My second date with Steven was the following Friday and it was even better than the first. It got off to a great start when my dad said we could stay out until 11:00 pm since it was a weekend night. I was nearly blown away since I thought he was going to say 10:00 pm but apparently he liked Steven enough to give us an extra hour. And if that wasn't enough, he gave me $50 and told me to have a good time. Anyway, Steven and I went to dinner at a local Mexican restaurant called Ixtapa, and just like our first date it was great fun. The food was awesome. I got a seafood burrito, Steven got chicken enchiladas, and we talked nonstop. But as far as I was concerned, the highlight of the night didn't happen until after dinner when we went to the mall to catch a movie. Steven let me pick it and of course I picked a chick flick, but to be honest since I was with him I would have been happy watching anything. We went to the concession stand, got some drinks and goodies, and took our seats. We laughed because my tub of popcorn was so big it almost needed a seat of its own, and his soda wasn't much smaller. Like always, the movie trailers started and there were so many of them that by the time they finished I had actually forgotten what movie we had paid to see. Anyway, we watched it for about half an hour, but then, for no real reason, I looked down from the screen and noticed Steven's hand was on the armrest between our seats, and it was less than an inch away from mine. I was a little hesitant at first, since I had never done anything like it before, but I took a deep breath, then reached over and took his hand in mine. Much to my delight, he clearly liked what I had done, and we spent most of the rest of the movie sitting there, holding hands. I was on cloud nine. The only time we stopped holding hands was when he decided to change things up and he put his arm around me, and as far as I was concerned that was even better than holding hands. While he had his arm around me, I leaned over and rested my head on his shoulder, which actually wasn't that comfortable since he had lean, bony shoulders, but I loved it anyway. I could have stayed like that all night, but unfortunately the movie came to an end and since it was almost 11:00 pm, he drove me home.

I was usually pretty humble, and I didn't really like to showboat or brag too much, but on that particular night I couldn't help myself. As soon as I got home I ran to my bedroom, jumped onto my bed, texted my teammates, and told them what had happened.

Riley was the first to respond. "Nice."

Then Erin responded. "He's a keeper."

Then Danielle responded. "You found a good one."

Then Kaitlin responded. "Does he have an older brother? If so, hook me up."

Much to her chagrin, I wrote back and told her there was no older brother. Steven's only sibling was Paige.

Anyway, I spent the next hour or so texting back and forth with them and it was great fun the entire time, but it got even better when Danielle sent the following message.

"Kissing is next."

My eyes got big the minute I saw the word 'kissing.' As you can probably guess, it made me a little nervous to think about it since I had never kissed a boy before, but at the same time, there was one thing I knew for certain.

I wanted to. And the boy I wanted to kiss, of course, was Steven.

The Fight

Our next Summer League game was one I would never forget. It was against a team from Mountlake Terrace called the Hawks, which I thought was kind of funny since it was the Hawks against the Skyhawks. Anyway, it started off like any normal game. I got a single during my first at-bat, then added a double during my second. In the meantime, Riley pitched and like usual did a great job. So we were all having fun and we were ahead 3-0 by the middle of the third inning. At that point, however, my attitude changed completely and I got a little depressed because a couple of the Hawks' players, including a stocky blonde who was their catcher, walked by and made some mean comments about me. The catcher imitated my voice, and the other girls laughed as soon as they heard her doing it.

"What were they thinking?" the catcher asked. "A deaf girl on a softball team? How stupid is that? What are they going to do next? Add a retard?"

Her comments stung, but like always I tried to ignore them, and it didn't really bother me too much until I got into the dugout, took a seat, and saw the girls across the field, still talking about me. They were too far away for me to hear them so I read their lips instead, which was probably a bad idea since I should have just ignored them and turned away. Anyway, the catcher said she would never want to be on a team with a deaf girl because to her being on a team with a deaf girl would be like being on a team with a bunch of morons and idiots.

I was so caught off guard and so depressed about what she had said I didn't even notice Riley was standing right next to me, looking at me.

"You okay?"

The minute I realized she was there, I turned to face her. "What?"

"You okay?" There was a look of concern in her eyes. "You don't look like yourself right now. You look like you're upset at something."

"It's nothing."

I didn't really want to tell her what was happening since it was pretty embarrassing. In addition, there was really no reason to tell her since there was nothing she could do about it anyway. Being teased by other girls was something I had always had to deal with, and even Riley herself had once made fun of me, way back during my first practice with the team.

But Riley, who was strong-willed and didn't like to take no for an answer, wanted to know what was bothering me.

"Tell me what's wrong, kid. Now."

I sighed. I didn't really know what to do and I didn't want to anger her, so I finally just came out and told her.

"Those girls are making fun of me. Especially the one in the middle, the catcher."

She looked across the field, at the three players, and her eyes narrowed the minute she saw them.

"Figures. The catcher is Evelyn Lavine. I've had issues with her before. Several times. She thinks she's the greatest thing since sliced bread. Don't worry. I'll take care of her."

She turned to walk away, but then stopped briefly and looked back at me.

"This isn't another trick, is it? Like the one you and Erin pulled on me against the LadyCats?"

I shook my head. "This isn't a trick. Not at all."

She nodded, then turned and walked away. A few minutes later, the game resumed and we took the field. But it didn't resume in any way I had ever imagined. By pure coincidence, the first batter was the Hawks' catcher, the stocky blonde Riley had referred to as Evelyn, and I watched from my spot in center field as the most amazing thing happened. Riley threw the first pitch right at her head. It didn't hit her, but only because she ducked down at the last second and somehow, miraculously, managed to get out of its path. She jumped back up, tossed her bat and helmet onto the ground, and started to walk toward Riley, who was standing in the pitching circle looking right at her.

"What was that for?" Evelyn yelled. Her face was red and she was furious Riley had thrown a pitch at her.

"That's for making fun of one of my teammates." Riley had left the pitching circle and was walking straight toward Evelyn. "Nobody makes fun of my teammates."

The umpire actually said something, but neither girl was listening to him, not at all, and they continued heading right for one another. Riley took off her mitt and threw it to the side.

"I can do whatever I want," Evelyn said.

"Not when I'm around," Riley said.

"Or what? What are you going to do?"

"I'll make you pay for it."

And then it got ugly. The girls were only a few feet apart, and Evelyn reached out and pushed Riley on the shoulder, and that was the wrong thing to do. Riley was a firecracker of a girl and she didn't back down from anything or anyone. Her response was a quick punch to the side of Evelyn's head, then one to her midsection. Evelyn responded by grabbing Riley by the hair, and they went down in a heap. Despite being the smaller of the two, Riley somehow ended up on top and she showed no mercy. She punched Evelyn again, this time in the face, then kneed her in the stomach.

I stood there in center field with my mouth wide open. I couldn't believe what I was seeing. I had never seen a fight during a softball game and I felt terrible about it. I felt like I had been the cause of the whole, ugly thing, and I regretted the fact I had told Riley anything about Evelyn teasing me.

Anyway, it took both coaches, both umpires, and several members of the field's grounds crew to break it up and finally pull the two girls apart. When they did, it was clear Riley had gotten the better of the whole thing. She had a nasty scratch on her left cheek, just below her eye, but other than that she looked okay. Evelyn, by contrast, was messed up bad. One of her eyes had already started to swell shut and she spit blood from her mouth. The home plate umpire ejected both of them from the game, then sent both teams to our dugouts for a few minutes so our coaches could calm everyone back down and regroup. I ran from center field to the dugout as fast as I could, first to make certain Riley was okay, then to apologize for what had happened. Riley was putting her stuff in her softball bag when I arrived, and she shot me a funny look as soon as I started to talk.

"Why are you apologizing?" she said. "You didn't do anything wrong. Evelyn was the one who started the whole thing. She was the one who made fun of you."

"But I got you ejected."

"You didn't get me ejected. I got myself ejected. It was my choice to challenge her. And it's no big deal. I'll be back tomorrow, at practice, and everything will be back to normal. And we'll have a really good story to tell."

I had never felt so relieved in my entire life. I had been petrified she would be upset with me. But quite to the contrary, she wasn't angry at all, and if anything she seemed completely the opposite. She was livelier than ever. She turned to Erin and the other girls and smiled brightly.

"That was an awesome fight. That was even better than the one last year against Bella Smith. Don't you think?"

I didn't know it at the time, but later that day the other girls told me about a game the year before when Riley had gotten in a fight with a girl named Bella Smith who played for the Bellevue Beast.

"There's no doubt about it," Erin said. "This one was way better. You messed up Evelyn bad. You gave her a black eye for sure."

"She should thank me. That black eye might make her look a little better."

Everyone laughed. We were about to continue talking but Russell walked up and said it was time for Riley to go so we could resume the game, so we all gave her hugs and off she went. Much to my delight, she walked away with a smile on her face. The last thing I heard as she headed for the parking lot was her voice as she said to herself, "Wow. I'm still filled with adrenaline. It's a complete rush."

From there the game resumed but it was pretty dull by comparison. Megan took over pitching for us and she gave up a run during her first inning, but other than that she did fine. We got three runs the next inning and the final score was 6-1. I got a single, in the bottom of the seventh, and I made two catches in center, but to be honest I didn't really care too much about that. All I cared about was the fight. For the rest of the game I kept thinking about it over and over in my mind and I couldn't help but smile. I couldn't believe how much things had changed in such a short period of time. Just a few weeks before, Riley had been the one who had made fun of me. But now she was the one who was defending me. As far as I was concerned, it didn't get any better than that.

On a related note, word must have spread around town about what had happened and clearly no one else ever wanted to face Riley's wrath, because no softball player ever teased me or made fun of me again.

Derrick

The following weekend was a big one for me. My dad got tickets to the Seahawks game on Sunday and I couldn't wait to go. I wasn't really a football fan and I didn't even know most of the rules, but I liked to go anyway because I got to see my favorite player, Derrick Coleman. Derrick was one of the Seahawks' fullbacks and he was really good, and he was my favorite player because he was the first person to ever play professional football who was legally deaf. Like me, he could hear a little, but only when he was wearing his hearing aids. Everyone in Seattle loved Derrick, but not just because he was a good player. In the off-season when the Seahawks weren't playing he went around town and did a lot of work for local charities, and he even gave hearing aids to children from needy families who couldn't afford to buy them for themselves. He also made appearances at schools and I got to meet him one year when he came to my school (I was in middle school back then) and he gave a speech in the gymnasium. He was super nice, and he talked about all of the challenges he had faced when he had been a kid, and how he had been bullied sometimes, which I thought was amazing since he was so big and strong I couldn't imagine anyone ever being able to bully him. His speech had been really inspirational and he had told us all to never give up, no matter what happened to us, no matter what challenges we faced, and of course I decided I wanted to be just like him.

The stadium was packed when we got there, and it was really lively like always since people in Seattle loved the Seahawks. We got drinks and hotdogs, then found our way to our seats and it was an exciting game. The Seahawks were playing the Chargers and the Chargers led for most of the game, but the Seahawks came back and won right at the end when the quarterback handed the ball to Derrick and he ran straight down the middle of the field. One of the Chargers' defenders tried to grab him by an arm, but Derrick was way too strong to be tackled like that, so he pulled away and broke into the clear. Two more Chargers tried to chase him down from behind but Derrick was way too fast to ever let that happen. The entire stadium went crazy and fireworks launched from the rafters as he dove into the end zone.

I was so happy I almost started to cry. As far as I was concerned, he was the greatest.

The Playoffs

The following Tuesday was a big day. The Summer League playoffs began, so the pressure really turned up a notch. From that point forward all of our games were do-or-die. If we won, we got to move on to the next round, and we still had a chance to make it to the championship game in Husky Stadium. But if we lost, our season was over and we could start making plans for next year.

Our game was against Seattle Fastpitch, which was a team we had played earlier in the year during pool play, and we were pretty confident we could win since we had beaten them 5-1 during our first game. Regardless, since there was so much at stake we were taking nothing for granted. We were serious and focused the whole time, and it was a good thing we were since Seattle Fastpitch put up a much better fight than they had during the first matchup. They jumped to a quick lead when they got back-to-back doubles in the first inning, but we came back in the second when Erin hit a single and Olivia hit a triple. For a few brief seconds, we all thought Olivia's hit was going to be a home run but it hit the top of the outfield fence and bounced back into play. Regardless, we were still happy and we took the lead momentarily when Riley hit a sacrifice fly that scored Olivia from third. Olivia is one of the bigger girls on the team, but trust me, she can fly when she needs to. Seattle Fastpitch's center fielder tried to throw her out at home plate but it wasn't even close.

From there, it was 2-1 until the fifth inning when Seattle Fastpitch's shortstop hit one down the left field foul line. Kaitlin dove in an attempt to get it, but she missed it by a hair and it went under her and rolled all of the way to the outfield fence. Like always, I ran over to back her up, but it took me quite a while to get there since the ball was so far away from me. Regardless, I grabbed it and whipped it in to Erin at short, but unfortunately the batter had already made it to third. The next batter hit a sacrifice grounder to Jamie at second. Jamie threw her out but was unable to do anything about the runner at third who scored easily.

I was getting a little nervous, since it was my first playoff game as a select player and I definitely didn't want it to be my last. In addition, I really wanted to play in Husky Stadium so I didn't even want to think about the possibility of losing and having our season come to a premature end.

Luckily, my worries were short lived. One of the nice things about being on a 16u select team was the fact I had older, more experienced girls on the team with me, and those older girls would take over when needed. Riley, Erin, and Danielle started the sixth inning by doing something I had never seen before, and to be honest I doubt I'll ever see it again. They hit back-to-back-to-back home runs and just like that we were ahead 5-2. In an attempt to stop the bleeding, Seattle Fastpitch's coach switched pitchers, but their backup wasn't even as good as their starter, and as such we quickly got another run when Kaitlin and Sophia hit doubles.

I didn't really do much, especially with my bat (I was zero for three), but I did make the final out to end the game. It was a simple pop up and anyone could have caught it, but regardless it felt really good when it landed in my mitt. Everyone said good catch and patted me on the back and before we knew it we were on to the second round.

Round Two

Our second game of the playoffs was even tougher than the first. It was against a team called the Kangaroos. I laughed when I heard the name, and I laughed even harder when I saw their symbol, which was a red kangaroo wearing oversized boxing gloves, but I wasn't laughing for long. Megan pitched for us and she did a good job but the Kangaroos were tough. Really tough. To me, they were the best team we'd played all year other than the Missfits. Their starting pitcher was an emo girl, which was somewhat strange to me since, in my experience, emo girls usually didn't like any sports other than skateboarding. Her name was Lillian Davies and she had short, dark hair with a cool, blue stripe on one side, pale skin, and black fingernails. She didn't throw very hard but she had a bunch of different pitches, including a riseball that was absolutely wicked. I had never seen a girl who could throw a riseball that well before. At first, it started low and looked like a normal fastball, but as it got closer it went higher and higher. She used it to strike out seven of our first nine batters. In the meantime, the Kangaroos' batters pounded out a couple of runs and by the beginning of the fourth inning we were down 2-0.

From there, we probably would have been doomed for sure if it hadn't been for Russell. He was an excellent coach and thankfully he had figured out a way to counter Lillian's riseballs.

"Don't swing at them."

"What do you mean?" Erin asked.

"Her riseballs aren't strikes. They're too high. So if you girls can stay patient and lay off of them, she'll be forced to stop throwing them."

It wasn't easy, since it was pretty hard to tell the difference between her fastballs and her riseballs, but we did our best and much to our delight Russell was right. Her riseballs were never strikes, so once we stopped swinging at them she was forced to throw different types of pitches instead. And when she started throwing different types of pitches, we started hitting them. Sophia led things off with a single in the fourth, then Danielle blasted a ball off of the fence in center. Sophia advanced to third, then scored when the next batter, Jamie, laid down one of the best drag bunts I had ever seen. The infielders rushed in to get it, but by the time they got there everyone was safe, including Sophia at home. I was the next batter and I popped out to second, but the batter after me, Olivia, hit a single that scored Danielle.

The game continued from there and it was a real nail biter. The Kangaroos scored two runs in the sixth to take a 4-2 lead, so it started to look pretty bleak for us again, but once again we didn't give up and we made a comeback. Olivia and Kaitlin hit back-to-back doubles to make it 4-3, and then Erin launched a massive home run to straightaway to give us a 5-4 lead. We clung to that lead until the bottom of the seventh and we won the game when Riley took over pitching for us and struck out all three batters she faced.

As I rounded up my stuff after the game, I could barely contain my excitement. We had made it all of the way to the semifinals, so all we had to do was win one more game and if we did, Husky Stadium was ours.

Date Number Three

Prior to our semifinal game, however, I had something really important to do - my next date with Steven. Like always, he picked me up at my house around 6:00 pm, but this date was a little different than its predecessors. On this date, we met some of his friends for dinner, two of which were boys I had met in Leavenworth, Peter and Wyatt. They had girls with them, so it was a group thing, and even though I would probably have preferred to have spent the entire time with Steven alone, I have to admit it was nice to get a chance to know his friends. We went to an Italian restaurant in Everett called The Vineyard and I got Fettuccine Alfredo, but to be honest it was pretty bland so I was a little disappointed. After dinner, we went to a bowling alley and had a blast. For a while we played singles and took turns, but then we split into teams and had a little competition, which of course Steven and I won easily. The other guys claimed it wasn't fair since Steven got to have me on his team.

"Why is that unfair?" he asked.

"Because," Peter said, "she's a big-time softball player. Look at those pipes on her. None of the other girls can compete with her."

At that, I got a little embarrassed because I realized what they were talking about. I was wearing a sleeveless top and they were all looking at my arms. I don't mean to sound conceited or anything, but my arms were really nice, both my triceps and biceps, and even without flexing you could see my muscles easily.

"My coach makes me do a lot of pushups," I said.

"We can tell," Peter said.

In an attempt to make the other boys happy, we mixed it up a little and they paired me with Peter, which of course I didn't like as much as being paired with Steven, but it was still fun. Peter and I won easily and the other girls looked a little miffed about it, since in essence I was showing them up, but at the same time they didn't seem to mind too much since it was just bowling after all.

The highlight of the date, however, and the part I had been waiting for all night, happened when Steven drove me home and dropped me off. Like normal, he pulled the car into my driveway, turned it off, and walked me to the front door. Unlike normal, however, he didn't just say goodnight, then turn and leave. Instead, he leaned forward, and ever so gently kissed me on the lips. It only lasted for a second but it made me feel incredible anyway. In addition, I think it made me greedy, because as soon as it was over I immediately wanted another. Anyway, after kissing me he said goodbye and turned and left, and I ran into the house as fast as I could. My dad was standing in the hall and tried to say something to me as I went by, but I was in too much of a hurry to even notice him. I had something much more important to do.

I had to text the other girls and tell them what had happened. I plopped onto my bed and started typing as fast as I could. And much to my delight their responses were immediate.

"Sweet," Erin wrote.

"Awesome," Riley wrote.

"Good 4 u," Olivia wrote.

But things got even better a few minutes later. Danielle wrote, "I'm looking at his Facebook page. You may want to look at it, too."

I didn't know why she would want me to do that, but I did anyway, and my eyes got big the minute it appeared on my screen. Steven had changed his "Personal" section to read, "In a relationship with Melody Gold."

"It's official," Danielle wrote. "You have a boyfriend."

The Semifinals

We were really excited about our next playoff game. If we won, we would advance to the championship game in Husky Stadium, which had been our primary goal all year. At the same time, however, we were nervous, since our opponent was a team from West Seattle called the Slammers. According to Russell, the Slammers were really good and they had won every one of their Summer League games easily, most by six or seven runs, some by more. As such, everyone expected an epic battle and a really good match-up.

Much to our surprise and delight, however, it wasn't. We took it to them right from the start. Five of our first six batters got hits, and before we knew it we were ahead 3-0. From there, we added two runs in the second, two in the third, and one in the fourth. In the meantime, Riley pitched the entire game and did a great job. The Slammers got one run off of her in the fifth inning, when their catcher hit a solo home run to left center, but other than that their efforts were fruitless. As such, we cruised to a surprisingly easy victory, and with it came our long-awaited invitation to Husky Stadium.

The Championship Game

The day of the championship game was a beautiful one and there wasn't a single cloud in the sky, which was rare in Seattle, even during the summer. Anyway, we were all excited since we finally got to play in Husky Stadium and it was an incredible experience. Husky Stadium was on the University of Washington's main campus, right next to Lake Washington, and the whole area was really pretty. You could see the lake in the distance, and on a day like that day, when the sun was out, the water sparkled brightly and there were fancy boats everywhere. The softball field itself was state-of-the-art, in every way, and we got there about two hours early just so we could take a look around and pose for photos. When we first got there, some of the University of Washington's players were still there since they had just finished their practice, and they said hi and wished us well in our game. Some of them even stayed to watch. I was in complete awe the moment they walked up and started talking to us, and I couldn't believe how big and strong they were. I bet some of them could hit home runs with only one arm if they had to.

Anyway, I was on top of the world because my dad and mom were there, as were my grandparents (they had driven all of the way from Spokane to see the game), and Steven, too. I introduced Steven to my grandparents, since it was the first time they had met him, and it was pretty exciting since it was the first time I had ever gotten to introduce him as "my boyfriend." My grandma, who had always been a spunky, little thing, made things even better when she looked at Steven, then turned to me and said, "Wow, young lady. You certainly know how to pick a cute one."

Needless to say, Steven was a big hit with everyone and he sat in the stands right next to my dad and grandpa. So everything was going perfectly until I started warming up with my teammates and looked across the field and saw who our opponent was.

At first, I couldn't believe my eyes. It was the Edmonds Express, the team that had refused to give me a spot because of my hearing impairment. At their front was their head coach, James Harbaugh.

My teammates saw me looking at them and instantly knew something was wrong.

"What's up, kid?" Riley asked.

Somewhat reluctantly, I told them the story, and their responses varied immensely from girl to girl.

Kaitlin was outraged. "They wouldn't take you because of your impairment? What a bunch of losers."

Jamie was shocked. "Who would do that? That's so lame."

Erin was grateful. "I'm glad they didn't take you. Had they, we wouldn't have gotten you."

Riley was motivated. "You helped me beat the Devils, which was the team that mistreated me. Now, I'm going to do the same for you. They're going to rue the day they met me."

And she wasn't kidding. She pitched like there was no tomorrow, which I guess was actually true (literally) since it was our last game of the season. She struck out six of the first seven batters she faced and she made three of them look foolish in the process (which was amazing, since the Express was a good team with a lot of good players). In the meantime, however, the Express' pitcher did an equally good job and she struck out six of our first nine batters, including me.

As such, it was a tense pitching duel right to the end. The only breakthrough happened in the bottom of the fifth inning. The Express' pitcher, who was a tall girl named Shera Williams, made a mistake and left a breaking ball over the plate and Erin crushed it. The ball sailed into the outfield stands and gave us a 1-0 lead.

As such, it was a great game and we were really happy since we had finally gotten the lead, but there was one thing that was a real drag.

Harbaugh. Like my hitting instructor, Steve, had originally told me, he was a complete idiot. He argued with the umpires all of the time, which was ironic, since they were doing a good job, and apparently he thought his mighty Express should have been able to beat us easily, so he continued to get more and more frustrated as they failed to do so. He started yelling at his players, more and more frequently as the innings wore on, and one girl, the center fielder, got a particularly nasty tongue lashing after Riley struck her out to end the fifth inning.

As I stood there watching Harbaugh yell at her, I felt bad for her, but at the same I was so relieved. I was so glad I was on the Skyhawks and not on the Express, since our coach, Russell, would never yell at one of us like that. Quite to the contrary, whenever we struck out, he usually ran up to us and gave us some tips how we could improve and avoid doing it again. I guess it's funny how things turn out sometimes. Back when I tried out for the Express and Harbaugh cut me, I was so upset and heartbroken I had started crying, but just a few months later I realized he had done me an enormous favor. He had led me to the Skyhawks, to the team where I belonged, and as far as I was concerned I was going to stay with them forever.

Unfortunately, however, disaster, at least as far as I was concerned, struck in the bottom of the sixth inning. We were up to bat and it was my turn. Shera got two quick strikes on me but then left a pitch over the plate and I hit it. Unfortunately, I didn't hit it very well and it ended up bouncing right to the Express' third baseman. She grabbed it and threw it to first but her throw was wild. In an attempt to catch it and keep it from flying out of play, the Express' first baseman stepped back and ended up right in my path as I was racing toward her. I was running so fast there was no way I could stop in time, and no way for me to dodge to the side. I ran right into her. Like most first basemen, she was a big girl, and it felt like I had run headfirst into a brick wall. We crumbled to the ground in a tangled mess of limbs the minute we hit, but, amazingly, that wasn't the worst of it. The ball arrived a second after we collided, and it nailed me right in the side of the head, right on my left ear. My batting helmet protected me from any serious damage, but even so it hurt so badly it instantly brought tears to my eyes. Russell, Harbaugh, and the two umpires ran onto the field to help both of us, and it was a good thing they did because we were both crying pretty hard by the time they arrived. I couldn't decide what hurt more, the side of my head where the ball had hit me or my left arm, since it had gotten smashed between us during the collision. In the meantime, the Express' first baseman was rolling around on the ground, holding her right knee with both hands, and I could tell she was in bad shape, too. It took several minutes for the coaches and umpires to calm us down, and I didn't really start to calm down for good until my dad came onto the field to help. Parents weren't normally allowed to come onto the field during games, but I guess they made exceptions in circumstances like that when players were injured.

"It's going to be okay, kiddo," my dad said. "You just need to take some deep breaths. Look right at me and take some breaths."

I did as instructed and amazingly, it worked. My head and my arm still hurt really badly, but at least I was finally able to calm down and stop crying.

Russell opened our team's medical kit and put an ice pack on my arm, then gave another to Harbaugh so he could put it on the first baseman's knee. A few minutes later we were both able to get back up, slowly, and the audience cheered as we did. As I turned to walk off of the field, I noticed my arm was feeling a little better, which was nice, but then I realized something different, and it was something that frightened me and stopped me dead in my tracks. I couldn't hear anything out of my left ear. I pulled off my helmet and removed my hearing aid, and the minute I saw it I knew instantly what the problem was. It was completely smashed. My helmet had saved me, but it hadn't been able to do anything for it. My dad took it from me and tried to fool with it for a while, to see if he could get it to work again, but I knew it was hopeless since it was basically nothing but pieces, and as a result I started to cry again because I knew I wouldn't be able to finish the game and Russell would have to replace me with one of our backup players.

Riley met me the minute I reached the dugout. "What do you mean? Why can't you finish the game?"

"I can't play with one hearing aid. When I wear just one, it irritates me and I get disoriented. Sometimes I get dizzy."

"We only have one inning left. Can you go that long?"

I shook my head. "I doubt it. And I don't want to risk making an error and blowing the whole game for everyone."

At the same time, however, I was completely heartbroken. Up to that point, I had played every inning of every game and I really wanted to stay on the field and complete the season.

"We need you on the field," Riley said. "You're our star center fielder, kid. We won't be the same without you."

I was extremely happy she had referred to me as 'our star center fielder' but even so I knew I was done.

"I can't do it. I'd like to, but I can't play with only one hearing aid."

Erin stepped forward with a solution. "Then play with none."

At first, I thought I had heard her wrong, which was completely possible since I was only wearing one hearing aid. "What? What do you mean?"

"Do you get disoriented when you take off both of your hearing aids?"

"No. I'm fine when I take them both off."

"Then take them off."

I looked at her with a funny look on my face. I was dumbfounded. "I won't be able to hear."

"You don't need to hear to play softball."

I was instantly skeptical and hesitant. I couldn't imagine playing softball without being able to hear anything.

Clearly, she saw my reaction and decided I needed some more persuading. "Melody, you're a good softball player because you work hard, you concentrate on your fundamentals, and you never give up. You're not a good softball player because you can hear. Like Riley said, we need you on the field with us. We know you can do it. Now you need to realize it, too."

I didn't know what to do so I turned to my dad, who was still in the dugout with us, just a few feet away, and he had overheard everything we had said. I was going to ask him what I should do but he spoke even before I got a chance to say anything.

"What have I always told you? What's our motto?"

The minute he said it, I knew exactly what he was talking about. "No excuses."

"Exactly. So take off that hearing aid before it starts to bother you and get back on the field. You have a championship to win."

I was pretty timid when I took my place in center field to start the next inning, but even so, I knew I had done the right thing. I thought briefly of my idol, Derrick, and I knew he would never quit a game just because he had broken one of his hearing aids. As such, I was determined to do my best, but it was a weird experience to say the least. I had never been on a softball field before without my hearing aids, and I was paranoid and a little afraid at first. From my spot in center I couldn't hear a thing and as a result everyone seemed like they were a million miles away. Even my fellow outfielders, Kaitlin and Sophia, who were to each of my sides, seemed so far away. In the distance, I could see the fans cheering, and the infielders shouting commands to one another, and the umpires discussing things, but I couldn't hear any of it. I tried my best to read people's lips, but it was hard to do since everyone was moving around so quickly. I started to feel a little better, however, when Riley finished her warmup pitches, turned, looked straight at me so I could see her lips clearly, and said, "Way to go, kid. Three outs and we win."

Much to my relief, things got off to a good start. It took five pitches, but Riley got the first batter to ground out to Jamie at second. Four pitches after that, she struck out the next batter. But then things got interesting. The next batter hit a shot right up the middle. For a minute, I thought Erin had a chance at it, but she couldn't get to it in time. The ball raced under her mitt and came to me in center. I moved in, scooped it up, and tossed it back to her.

It was a routine play, about as simple as one could get, but it made all of the difference in the world. For some strange reason, the minute I touched that ball and felt its seams against my fingertips, my attitude changed completely. Just a few seconds prior, I had been timid and afraid, and I had had serious doubts about whether I could make a play at all. But now that I had, I knew I could, and I readied myself for whatever would happen next.

And it was a good thing I did. The Express' next hitter was a monster of a girl named Hannah Livingston. She was one of the biggest girls I had ever seen, at least six feet tall and probably two hundred pounds. If someone had told me she was a linebacker for Jackson's football team I would have believed it. But despite her size, Riley wasn't intimidated at all, and what followed was one of the best pitcher/batter battles I had ever seen. Riley threw every pitch in the book, and every one of them was nasty, and a normal batter would have been destroyed for sure. But not Hannah. She was a great hitter and she managed to stay alive and foul away pitch after pitch after pitch after pitch. I stopped counting after the tenth. But finally my eyes got big and my heart skipped a beat as Riley made the perfect pitch, low and away, right across the outside corner of the plate, and I thought Hannah was done for sure. Quite to the contrary, however, she reached out and hit it. And she didn't just hit it. She crushed it. I knew it was trouble the minute it left her bat. It was heading for the gap in left center, exactly half way between Kaitlin and me, and it was going there faster than I could believe possible. Kaitlin was a great softball player and an excellent outfielder but she wasn't super fast so I knew there was no way she could get to it in time. As such, I knew I had to get it, and I knew I had to get it before it hit the ground or the runner on first would score for sure. Normally, I prefer to turn on my afterburners and catch hits like that on the run, but this one was just too far away and it was tailing away quickly. I was already going full speed, but even so I knew there was no way I could run under it in time.

So I did the only thing possible.

I dove.

Normally, I didn't like diving, since it hurt, and that time was no exception. I flew at least ten feet through the air, maybe more, with my arms stretched out as far as possible in front of me, and I hit the ground at the very second the ball went into my mitt. At first, I didn't know if I had caught it or not, and to be honest I didn't really care since I hit the ground so hard it knocked the wind out of me and actually stunned me for a second. When I finally recovered and I tried to get back up, I noticed the field umpire had run up to me and he was shouting something, but I couldn't hear him so I read his lips instead.

"Show me your mitt. Show me your mitt."

It actually took a second for things to fully register, since I was still recovering and my ribs were hurting so badly I could barely lift my arms above my waist, but I raised my mitt in front of him, opened it, and my heart stopped as I saw what was inside.

"It's a catch," he said. "The batter is out. The game is over."

After that, it was pure pandemonium. From the pitching circle, Riley fell (literally) onto her back and started crying tears of joy. Jamie and Erin hugged one another and Kaylee threw her mitt as high into the air as it would go. Kaitlin and Sophia rushed up and were about to pile on top of me in celebration, but at the last second they saw I was cradling my arm and my ribs and they decided they better take it easy on me instead. They patted me on the back, gave me hugs, and walked me to the dugout where Russell and the assistant coaches were celebrating. It was great fun, possibly the best time I had ever had, and a few minutes later things got even better when the Summer League's tournament director, who was an elderly man named Fred Williamson, came over and gave us a shiny trophy and some sweet T-shirts. They were green and gold and said "Summer League Champions" on the front. The only bad thing, however, was we had to cut our celebration short because Russell and my dad saw me struggling to get my shirt on, which I couldn't do since I was unable to raise either of my arms above my shoulders, and they both got worried I had broken my ribs. As such, they insisted on taking me to the nearest hospital for x-rays and I didn't really object since I was hurting pretty badly. Luckily for me, however, my ribs weren't broken, but the doctor said they were bruised badly and would need several weeks to recover. When I finished my exam and headed back out to the hospital's waiting area, I was pretty touched to see all of my teammates sitting there, lounging on the couches waiting for me. They all wanted to make certain I was okay and they had even chipped in and bought me some flowers and balloons. Steven was there with them, and even though I was still in a lot of pain, it made me feel great to see him.

The End of the Season

We had our end-of-the-season party the following weekend. By then, I had gotten new hearing aids and my arm and ribs had largely recovered, which I was grateful for since the prior week had been tough. Trust me, you never want to have bruised ribs because even a simple thing like laughing hurts. Anyway, the party was at a pizza place in Federal Way, not too far from our practice field, and I was actually a bit depressed when we got there. I had enjoyed being on the Skyhawks so much I didn't want the season to come to an end and I couldn't believe how quickly it had happened. My first practice with the team seemed like it had just been the day before. As such, it took the other girls quite a while to cheer me back up.

"Next season will be here faster than you can imagine," Erin said. "And then we'll be back in action."

"And next season is going to be even better than this one," Danielle said.

I raised an eyebrow. This year had been pretty good, with us winning the Summer League championship and all. I didn't see how it could get any better than that.

"Hasn't anyone told you?" Danielle asked. "Russell is already making arrangements for a road trip next year. And guess where we're going. Hawai'i."

My heart raced the minute she said it. "Really? They have tournaments in Hawai'i?"

"Of course. They have tournaments everywhere."

I liked the sound of that. This year's road trip to Leavenworth had been great and I had met Steven there so I doubted a future road trip could ever top that, but even so Hawai'i sounded pretty good to me. I had never been there and going there with the Skyhawks to play a tournament would be unforgettable. So from that point forward I was in a good mood again. We got pizza, and we joked around and had fun, and at one point Russell gave an end-of-the-season speech and handed out a bunch of trophies. Kaylee won the Gold Glove award for the team's best defensive player, Riley won the Silver Slugger award for the team's best hitter, Danielle won Most Inspirational Player, and Erin won Most Valuable Player. I didn't win any awards but to be honest I didn't really want any, since all that mattered to me was the fact I had found a team and I had been able to prove that, despite having a hearing impairment, I could contribute and help the team win. To me, that was reward enough.

Glossary of Key
Softball Terms

At-bat: A player's turn to bat while her team is on offense. Players take turns batting. In a typical seven inning game, a player will usually get three or four at-bats.

Batting Order: The order in which batters take turns hitting during a game. The batting order is usually chosen by the team's coach or its manager at the beginning of the game. The batter who bats first is called the 'leadoff hitter,' and the fourth batter is called the 'cleanup hitter.' Many players see it as a promotion to be moved up in the order (closer to the leadoff batter), since they will get more at-bats per game, and they see it as a demotion to be moved down in the order.

Ball: A pitch that travels outside of the strike zone that the hitter does not swing at. If a pitcher throws four balls to a batter, before she gets three strikes, it results in a walk.

Blue: An informal term used to refer to the umpires. It originates from the traditional color of their uniforms.

Bunt: A soft hit produced by holding the bat in a stationary position over home plate. Bunts are often used strategically to advance a base runner to the next base. There are several different types of bunts, including 'sacrifice bunts' and 'push bunts.' During a sacrifice bunt, the batter intentionally tries to bunt the ball in a way so the defensive players will throw her out at first, thus allowing a base runner to advance safely to the next base. During a push bunt, a batter tries to reach first base safely by pushing the ball between the defenders just out of their reach.

Change-up: A pitch that is thrown to a batter much slower than a pitcher's other pitches. It is also called a 'change.'

Count: The term used to describe a batter's balls and strikes during her at-bat. The number of balls is listed first, followed by the number of strikes. If blue says, "The count is two and one," he's telling everyone the batter has two balls and one strike.

Curveball: A pitch that curves as it heads toward home plate.

Double play: A play in which the defense records two outs. If the same player makes both outs, with no help from any other player, it is called an 'unassisted double play.'

Error: A ruling charged to a defensive player if she makes a mistake that should have resulted in an out.

Fair ball: A ball that, when hit, lands between the two foul lines and stays in bounds past first or third base. A home run is considered a fair ball.

Fastball: A type of pitch thrown to a batter. It is usually extremely fast (thus, the name).

Fastpitch: Fastpitch is a type of softball where the pitcher is allowed to pitch the ball as hard and as fast as she wants. In slowpitch softball, the pitcher is not allowed to throw the ball hard.

Fielders: The players who are playing defense and trying to get the batters and runners out.

Fly ball: A ball that is hit high into the air and is usually caught by the defenders.

Fly out: A ball that is caught by one of the defensive players before it touches the ground. The batter is out as soon as the ball is caught.

Force out: After a batter hits the ball, she must advance to first base. The defensive players can get her out by throwing the ball to first base before she reaches it. Additionally, other base runners must advance to the next base if they are forced by a base runner behind them.

Foul ball: A ball hit outside of the two foul lines. It results in a strike. If a batter already has two strikes when she hits a foul ball, the count remains the same and the at-bat continues, because a foul cannot result in a strikeout. A 'foul tip' is a type of foul ball that is hit directly behind the batter.

Ground ball: A ball hit on the ground in the infield.

Ground-rule double: A hit that lands in fair territory and bounces over the outfield fence. The batter is awarded second base, and all of the runners who were on base at the time advance two bases.

Hit: A batted ball that allows the batter to safely reach base. There are several types of hits. A single is a hit that allows a batter to advance to first base. A double is a hit that allows the batter to advance to second. A triple is a hit that allows a batter to advance to third base, and a home run is a hit that allows the batter to advance all the way to home plate.

Hit and run: A play where the base runner advances to the next base as soon as the pitcher releases the ball. Usually, the batter attempts to hit the ball regardless of whether it is a ball or a strike.

Home run: A hit that allows the batter to reach home plate safely. There are several types of home runs. An out-of-the-park home run is a hit that flies over the outfield fence between the two foul poles. The batter and any runners that are on base at the time are awarded home plate and each of them scores a run. An inside-the-park home run is a hit that does not fly over the outfield fence, but the batter reaches home plate anyway. A solo home run is a home run that occurs when there are no base runners on base, and a grand slam is a home run that occurs when there is a base runner on first, second, and third bases. In Seattle, a grand slam is called a 'Grand Salami' — a term coined by the legendary sportscaster Dave Niehaus.

Inning: The individual segments of a game. Each game has seven innings. Each team gets to bat once during each inning, and it gets to continue batting, and scoring runs, until the other team makes three outs. The visiting team bats first, in what is called the 'top' of the inning, and the home team bats second, in the 'bottom' of the inning.

Line drive: A ball that is hit very hard and with a trajectory almost parallel to the ground. Players are taught to hit line drives, because it is often very difficult for the defensive players to catch them.

No-hitter: A game in which the pitcher does not allow the opposing team to get any hits. No-hitters are extremely rare, and they are seldom done by any player at any level.

Out: The defense must create three 'outs' before an inning is over.

Power hitter: A batter who is known for hitting the ball extremely hard.

Riseball: A type of pitch that starts low, like a fastball, but rises dramatically as it heads toward home plate. Many batters (including Fastpitch Fever's star, Rachel Adams) are fooled by riseballs and they swing too low and miss them.

Robbed: A term used by players to describe a play in which they lose a hit, usually because a defensive player makes an outstanding play. In Fastpitch Fever, Rachel Adams was robbed of a hit in the state's championship game when the opposing center fielder dove and caught the ball. The girl who inspired *Fastpitch Fever*, Molly McCall, was robbed on a daily basis.

Run: A run is scored when a base runner safely reaches home plate.

Sacrifice: A play where a batter intentionally hits the ball into an out situation so she can advance or score a runner.

Safe: A ruling made by blue when a base runner safely reaches a base.

Screwball: A pitch that curves toward the side of the plate from which it was thrown.

Slapper: A left-handed batter known primarily for using her speed to get to first base.

Stolen base: A play in which a runner advances safely to the next base as soon as the pitcher releases the pitch.

Strike: A pitch that a batter swings at and misses, hits foul, or fails to swing at that crosses the strike zone. A batter is out after receiving three strikes.

Strike out: A play when a batter accumulates three strikes, at which point her at-bat ends and she is out.

Strike zone: The area above home plate between a batter's knees and armpits.

Tag out: A play in which a fielder with the ball tags a base runner who is not standing on a base.

Tag up: A base runner cannot leave a base until a batted ball hits the ground. If she does, and if the ball is caught, she must return to her base. If she waits until the ball is caught, then leaves the base, the play is called a 'tag up' and she is allowed to go.

The Cycle: A term used by players to describe the 'holy grail' of softball. A player hits for the cycle when she hits a single, double, triple, and home run in the same game. It is extremely hard to do and rarely done by any player at any level. The girl who inspired *Fastpitch Fever*, Molly McCall, hit for a 'super cycle' during one of her Little League games: she hit a single, double, triple, home run, and she was intentionally walked by the opposing pitcher.

Triple play: A play in which the defense records three outs. If the same player makes all three outs, with no help from any other players, it is called an 'unassisted triple play.' Triple plays are extremely rare.

Walk: Four balls from a pitcher results in the batter receiving a 'walk,' and the batter automatically advances to first base. A walk is also referred to as a 'base on balls.' An 'intentional walk' is a type of walk where the pitcher intentionally throws four balls, and she does not even try to get the batter out. Intentional walks are done to avoid pitching to really good batters in key situations.

About the Author

Jody Studdard is the author of several children's novels, including *Kiana Cruise: Apocalypse*, *Fastpitch Fever*, *Escape from Dinosaur Planet*, and *The Sheriff of Sundown City*. He is a graduate of Monroe High School (1989), the University of Washington (1993), and California Western School of Law (1995). In addition to writing, he is a practicing attorney with an office in Everett, Washington. He is a fan of the Seahawks, Storm, Sounders FC, and Kraken.

E-mail Jody at:

jodystuddard@gmail.com

Made in the USA
Las Vegas, NV
06 December 2021